T0367242

ASYLUM

ASYLUM

B.J. Andres

ASYLUM

iUniverse books may be ordered through booksellers or by contacting:

iUniverse
1663 Liberty Drive
Bloomington, IN 47403
www.iuniverse.com
1-800-Authors (1-800-288-4677)

ISBN: 978-1-5320-6834-8 (sc)
ISBN: 978-1-5320-6835-5 (e)

Print information available on the last page.

iUniverse rev. date: 02/07/2019

CHAPTER 1

"No! No! No! NOOOOO! You can't take me in there! Get your damn hands off of me! Baby, don't let them take me in there! You said I was just coming to talk . . . why? Why are you letting this happen?" At 9:32 on a crisp, October morning, two men dressed in white uniforms dragged a crying and writhing man from the passenger seat of a black car that was parked outside the Euphoria Hills Institution. He had been coerced into getting into the car by his crafty wife back at their home. He fought with all his might, but couldn't match the power of the two men that held onto him. The man looked behind him at his wife with pleading eyes, "why baby . . . why are you doing this to me . . . to us?" She stood by the car silently, staring at the ground with tears rolling down her rouged cheeks. The men took him through the sanitarium's heavy doors, and they slammed shut with a dominant thud. He belonged to them now. The salt and pepper haired doctor, and a petite, blue-eyed blond haired woman stayed outside with his wife to get the new patients medical history, allergies and other information. The blond, who was the head nurse, rushed inside to aid the orderlies in their attempt to sedate the unruly man after all of the important details had been taken. The doctor put his hand on the wife's shoulder as gesture of your *'husband is in good hands'*. At that, she quickly turned to get into the driver's seat, and sped away from the

1

nightmare she had experienced. The wife of the man had left him in the so called trusting hands of complete strangers.

Inside the hospital, the new patient continued his attempt to dominate the hospital staff, but was given a calming medicine by injection and strapped to a bed. By the time the doctor was given the chance to see him, he was intoxicated from the medication. The doctor hovered over the man bound to the bed. He looked into his half-lid, brown eyes and didn't bother addressing him directly.

"What and how much was he given for his acute psychosis?" The doctor asked the head nurse. She was the one that took down all of the important information, and would know these details.

"He was given five milligrams of Haldol." The nurse quickly skimmed the chart. "Two milligrams of Ativan by injection . . . and you know the rest, Dr. Krochek." She responded, hushing her voice.

"All right, give him until the day after tomorrow. Then I'll speak to him. If he becomes agitated before I have the chance to talk to him, administer a B52." He said sternly, and then whirled around, and exited the room. The head nurse quickly followed the doctor. All that were left in the room was an orderly, and the new arrival.

"This place isn't so bad. The doc is going to talk to you a couple times, and then you're going to be put into a deep sleep. You'll then have the bestest best dream of your life. It's going to feel real too, you know? I know, because I was a tester a few years back when the technology was first brought in here. You have nothing to worry about man. Trust me. It will all be over just as soon as it begins." The orderly patted the man on the shoulder, smoothed his sandy blond hair back and stood up. "Get some sleep, I have worked here for almost ten years, and have only seen . . . two people . . . discharged in that time. Once you're here . . . you are in for the long haul. Not trying to sound like a jerk, just being honest. Good night." The orderly got up from the green, plastic chair and kicked it back against the wall without turning around. He began to whistle an unfamiliar tune, turned out the light, and shut the door to the room. The man was left alone in the almost void space. He tried his hardest to fight against the padded restraints that held him to the uncomfortable bed. No matter how much strength he managed to muster, his attempts were to no avail. He tried to yell, but could only manage a diminutive moan in the back of his throat.

The drugs had rendered him useless. He could feel the salty tears and drool stream down his face, and pool inside of his ear. He was losing control of his own body, and he could feel himself slipping into an abyss of despair in his mind. But as quickly as these profound feelings of misery arrived, the emotional turmoil suddenly disappeared. It was replaced by feelings of calming warmth. His whole body began to tingle, and a sound like white noise mixed with a ringing drowned out the sound of rushed footsteps, demented laughter, and short screams in the hallway outside of his door. His dark room was filled with an array of different colors that were made of pixilated dots. His body and mind began to feel lighter than air. He started to feel like he was floating away from the bed, and he was no longer in the hospital. His eyelids began to feel heavier, and he was in a trance by the colors moving in a swaying motion around him. A smile was impossible because the medicine seemed to have paralyzed his muscles. He closed his eyes to enjoy the weightless feeling and the fog his mind was in. Soon enough, everything went dark in his mind, and he was fast asleep. He had given in to the medication, and he was at the mercy of the hospital staff.

He had slept for twenty-six hours straight, and dreamed about nothing. He saw nothing but darkness as he slept. When he awoke, he was still tethered to the bed. He let out a sound of dismay when he realized he had urinated in the bed as he slept. "Hey! Is anyone out there?" He croaked in a raspy voice.

'They will all ignore you.' A voice in his head whispered. His throat was dry and scratchy. He tried licking his cracking lips, but it was pointless. *'They have forgotten about you. I'm the only one who cares for you.'* The voice whispered again. The man ignored the voice. His main concern was trying to get the attention of someone that would get him off of the bed, and maybe let him walk around, get a shower and a drink. He felt stiff from lying in the same position for as long as he had, and his mouth felt like he had been chewing on cotton balls. He thrashed violently against the padded restraints that held him to the sheet covered, plastic mattress.

"Helloooo!" He pathetically shrieked. He finally heard footsteps outside, and the door opened slightly. A quiet and gentle female voice was finally heard.

"Can I help you?"

"Yeah, Can someone tell me what's going on . . . maybe let me outta these things?" He asked as he pulled up on the padded restraints.

"I'll have to check with your doctor first. You also need to see the physician for an intake physical." She said, as she opened the door the rest of the way. The light from the hallway flooded the room. He wasn't expecting it, and winced from the brightness.

"Can I least get outta these straps to go to the bathroom, please? Maybe some water? Can I least get a shower and some clean clothes?" The nurse left for a brief moment, and came back with a plastic cup that had a paper straw hanging from it.

"I can't let you out of the restraints until your doctor signs off on it. It's protocol." She held the straw to his lips, and allowed him to drink until the cup was dry.

"So, I'm supposed to just . . . lie here in my own piss?" He was getting aggravated and the nurse was barely giving him any answers. The nurse put the cup aside on a small table with wheels, grabbed hold of his wrist, and looked at her digital watch to take a pulse reading. She scribbled something on the chart in her hand disregarding his question. "Are you just going to ignore me?" It stayed silent between the two until the nurse decided to speak to him.

"I will be back in to take your blood pressure and temp." She quickly walked out of the room, and left the door open a crack. She was only gone a few minutes when she returned to the room. This time she turned the lights on inside the room. The man closed his eyes tightly, and let out a sigh of dismay from the sudden change. He blinked his watery eyes to adjust to the high definition lights. The red headed nurse was dressed in a white uniform like the men who had dragged him inside upon his arrival, except she wore a skirt, and her name tag read LPN. She added a wool sweater for her own comfort. She had large, brown doe eyes that made her appearance innocent. "What is your approximate weight?" She asked as she pulled out a small, hand-held machine from her blue sweater pocket.

It had three wires that came off of it. A red wire would measure his systolic pressure, and a blue wire would measure his diastolic. These wires together also did an EKG. A green wire would measure his body temperature and pulse.

4

"I'm about one-ninety-five" The man told the nurse, trying to be cooperative. She retrieved three disposable electrodes from the back of the machine, and attached the wires on the left side of his chest over his heart. She pressed some buttons on the small machine in her hand, it vibrated a couple times, and he felt a slight tingle from the wires on his chest. After two minutes passed, a long beep was heard from the machine.

"All done! One fifty over a hundred ten is your blood pressure and ninetyeight point eight is your temp. Your blood pressure is a little high." She wrote it down on the same chart as his pulse." The physician will take his own measurements when he sees you later on, but for now just relax." She told him, as she removed the electrodes, and pulled the wires from the little machine to discard them.

"Relax . . . how does one do that in this shit show?" He snorted. The nurse disregarded the question. She turned off the light, and closed the door as she left without saying a word. Once again, he was left alone in the dark, except this time he had no drugs to make him feel at ease and to help him drift off to the land of colors again. He began to realize that no one here truly cared about the patients. It was just a job to them. He was just a job. Patient number . . . whatever. The staff would never know him by his name. They all went home, and had fun, weekend barbeques on their days away from work. They didn't give anyone here a single thought, unless it was to tell a funny story about the patient who snapped and threw shit at the wall. These thoughts agitated him, and he was filled with an overwhelming feeling of hostility. He didn't want to be there anymore. He was sure he didn't belong there, despite of the issues he had. He had been managing them fine on his own. He wasn't even there for the full experience, but what he had witnessed already was enough. The cold and withdrawn behavior of the staff was enough to send the sanest person on a homicidal rampage. Not one person had made true eye contact with him to make him feel like a human being. The orderly he met when he first arrived did nothing but taunt him slightly. His doctor stood over him, and observed the man as if he was another specimen under a microscope. He felt the hot tears of aggravation forming in his eyes from the anger. He squeezed his eyes closed to try and stop them from falling, and eventually succeeded.

"I know you're there you son of a bitch." He said out loud suddenly.

"Don't you think for a second that you won just because I'm in this hell hole. You'll never get what you want from me." A black, lanky shadow in the corner cowered down, and two red balls of fiery light disappeared.

He tried to sleep to pass the time, but found himself thinking about a million things at once. His business, his wife, his house . . . what was to come of the life he had worked so hard to build? Three hours passed, and a different nurse came in. She flicked on the lights and walked towards the window.

"Rise and shine!" She said in an obnoxiously cheerful way.

"I wasn't asleep." The man mumbled quietly.

"What was that?" The nurse asked boisterously as she flung open the curtains to bare the mid afternoon sun.

"I said . . . I wasn't . . . fucking . . . ASLEEP!" He repeated more loudly and with more volatility. He had hours to lie there, and grow more angry and hostile with his thoughts.

"Come now, don't be like that! We're all friends in here!" The nurse said spiritedly.

"A friend wouldn't leave a friend strapped to a bed like this. I've been lying in this damn bed, in my own filth for . . . God only knows how long. You all have fun shooting me up with drugs against my will?" He said heatedly. He felt the hostility rising even more. No one had been back in since the nurse that brought him the water. He had not eaten since he was in the hospital.

"Well, that's what I'm here for. The physician wants to see you." She took a syringe and an alcohol pad from her front pocket. She cleaned an area on the man's arm and stuck him with the needle. "Don't worry, it's just a mild sedative. It's procedure with all the patients that have been in isolation, but I'm still taking those straps off! So, that's good news!" She explained enthusiastically as she began to undo the straps. "I guess that makes us friends now." She said when she finished unbuckling the last strap. Her perky attitude about his situation was getting on the man's nerves. Instead of saying anything, he took a deep breath, and tried to sit up by himself, but found that he couldn't. The nurse smiled thinly at him, and let out a small, arrogant laugh. She tucked her arm under his back, and helped him sit up. When he was upright, his head began to spin, and he wanted to fall back against the pillow again.

"I feel like I'm drunk or high in a bad way or something. What did you people give me?" The man said raspily. "Can I get some clean clothes and a shower?"

"That feeling should eventually wear off, but for now . . ." The nurse's voice trailed off, and that's when he noticed the wheelchair in the room.

"Is that . . . for me? You gave me something that really messed me up." He said resentfully.

"Yes, you won't be able to walk very well without assistance. There are always consequences for our negative actions. We are going to make a pit stop at the bathroom for you." She said quickly with a big, fake smile that showed all of her cheesy teeth. He managed to get his legs over the edge of the bed by himself. The nurse helped him stand, and he took three small sliding steps to the wheelchair. He turned and sat with a grunt. He had never felt more helpless. The nurse unlocked the brakes, and wheeled him out of the room. They went down a long, white corridor lined with doors on both sides. Every door was closed and had a number on it, except for two which had gender specific signs. They stopped at the mens door, and a male orderly came to assist him.

Once he was finished in the bathroom, he was placed in the wheelchair again. They proceeded on the journey to the doctor's office. They approached some windowless double doors at the end of the hall, and the nurse pulled at her name tag which also doubled as a key card. The doors opened and she pushed him through them. On the other side of the double doors, it was basically the same thing . . . more doors lining each side of a long white, brightly lit hallway, and all of the doors were closed. Except, in this hallway, these doors were labeled "STORAGE" and "DR. WAGNER," among other names. At the end of this hallway, there was another set of windowless double doors that you didn't need a key card to open. There were small intercoms next to the doors that were labeled for the doctors. They were accompanied with cameras that had a plexiglass case protecting them with small opening in them for pushing the buttons to notify the doctor inside of the office. She pushed the wheelchair to the fourth door on the right-hand side, and came to an abrupt halt that almost knocked the man from the wheelchair. The nurse put her finger through a hole in the plexiglass, and pushed a small white button on the intercom. A buzzing sound was heard from behind the door. The man noticed the camera lens move toward his face and look at him. This made him feel uneasy, and he quickly looked away from it and put his focus on the name on the door.

'Dr. Montgomery . . . who is this guy?' The man thought to himself. A static voice came through the intercom.

"Hello. What is the patient number?" A male voice asked. The nurse pulled a chart from the back of his wheelchair and flipped it open.

"Patient number, 0043790172." She answered methodically.

"Okay, proceed through, please." The intercom's static ceased as it disconnected. A heavy clicking sound was heard, and the door opened. A man sat behind an oversized oak desk with a large window behind him that had the curtains open. A built in book case lined the one wall. Behind the doctor's desk in the corner, on a small table, sat a working antique radio. There was an exam table on the other side of the room placed at an angle, which allowed a medical supply cart to fit against the wall beside it. There was a locked closet in the corner by the exam table. The carpet was dark red with small black diamonds placed in an even and parallel pattern. There were small tears in it from wheeling heavy equipment around. The wall that wasn't adorned with a book case had the top half decorated with a dark-green wall paper that was vertically striped with a lighter green color. The bottom half was made of a dark wooden wainscoting. The interior design of the room clashed in a nauseating way. The nurse pushed him up to the desk, and placed the brakes on the wheelchair. The only light in the room was from the small table lamp on the doctor's desk, and the sunlight that came in from the large window behind his desk. The glare from the sun made it hard for the man to make out any facial features of the doctor. He could see he had black hair that he kept parted neatly off to the left side. The doctor was typing on a hologram computer.

"Would you like me to stay in here or wait outside Dr. Montgomery?" The nurse asked.

"Considering this is his first exam, and the medications he was given, I think you should stay." She handed the physician the man's chart. He reached for a pair of black, plastic framed glasses, and placed them on the end of his nose with one hand. "All right, let's see here. We're still in the process of transferring all of your information to an electronic tablet." He glanced over the chart for thirty seconds and snapped it shut with force.

"Okay, I am going to get your blood pressure, pulse and temperature. I'm also going to have you do your best attempt at a standard physical. Do you understand what I am saying to you right now?" The doctor asked the man.

"What . . . do you think English is my second language or something?" He replied with a smirk. This comment caught the doctor off guard, and he looked at the man over his glasses for a moment. He thought about coming back with something as equally witty, but decided against it. Instead of feeding into the patient's sarcasm, he reached into the top left desk drawer, and pulled out the same device that the nurse used on him earlier when he was still strapped down to his bed. He set it on his desk, and stood up.

"I'm going to take your weight so I can get an accurate blood pressure." He motioned to the nurse to help him stand the patient up. She walked over and the two of them walked him over to what looked like a treadmill with long railings. "Hold onto those railings for support as much as you want. We will still get an accurate weight." Dr. Montgomery advised. The man did as he was told, and in thirty seconds, a robotic female voice announced that he weighed one hundred and ninety-three pounds. The nurse helped him back into the wheelchair, and put him back in front of the desk. The nurse bared the man's chest through the hospital gown for easy access for the wires. The doctor put on a pair of nitrate gloves, and pulled three electrodes from the dispenser in the back of the machine. He attached three new wires to the machine, and the other ends of those same wires to the left side of the man's chest with the electrodes. The doctor punched some buttons on the handheld machine in his hand and it vibrated a couple times just as it did before. He felt the same slight tingle from the wires. Two minutes later, the same long beep was heard. The doctor reached for the man's chart and scrawled his findings down, and disconnected the three wires from the man and the machine. He threw the used electrodes and wires into the trash and placed the device back into the desk drawer. "So far, so good. If we could get you over to the exam table, I would like to check your reflexes, lungs, and all that good stuff." Once again, the doctor and nurse aided the man. He was given a thorough physical by being attached to an array of different handheld devices, and put back in the wheelchair. "Your lungs and everything else looks good considering you were a habitual marijuana smoker and drank as much as you did. Your blood pressure is a bit high, but your EKG looks fine. Are you stressed out about anything?" The doctor asked.

"Seriously? Am I stressed out? Well where should I begin doc?" The man responded sarcastically.

"Okay, okay. I get it. Not having the best of times right now. My advice . . . you should take this time to relax. You have no responsibilities, and all you have to worry about . . . is you." The doctor pointed at the man. "It's like a vacation almost."

"Yeah . . . because I was just thinking the other day how nice a trip to the nut hut would be! You know . . . lie around in a piss margarita . . . do some mystery drugs that make you see colors that weren't invented yet. Hey doc, have you ever tasted purple?" He rolled his eyes. Dr. Montgomery saw he wasn't going to get very far with the patient at the moment.

"Well, you're free to go." The doctor said with a sigh.

"Yup, another one that doesn't really give a shit." The man mumbled under his breath.

"What was that?" Dr. Montgomery asked.

"Nothing. I didn't say anything." The man proclaimed. "Say doc, are you hearing things? Because if that's the case . . ."

"All right, that's enough." Nurse Adams interrupted. "Dr. Montgomery . . . as always, it's been a pleasure." She took the handles of the wheelchair, and directed the man out of the office.

"Am I going to be strapped down to my bed again?" He asked the nurse a few seconds later. She didn't answer him. He figured she didn't hear him. He asked the question again. "Am I going to be strapped down to my bed again?" He was still given no response. Frustrated wasn't even the word to describe what he was now. After everything he had already been through, being ignored wasn't something he was prepared to deal with again, and this nurse was really trying his patience. *'Why can't she just answer the question?'* He screamed to himself. Suddenly, an idea came to him. He placed his hands on the arms of the wheelchair, and pushed up and over with all his might. He threw his entire body on the cold, tile floor with a flop. "One more time! I ASKED . . . am I going to be strapped down again?" The nurse looked down at the helpless man lying on the floor, and smiled her yellow toothed grin again.

"Well, now you are." She pulled at a thick, silver chain around her pale neck that was hidden by her stiff collar. Attached to it was a long, thin silver whistle that she blew into that caught the attention of two stocky orderlies. They came at a rapid pace, and the nurse pointed to the man. "Have a nurse administer a B52, and put him in his bed restraints until he sees Dr. Krochek tomorrow." It was at this moment he saw her name tag, and it read HEAD NURSE. She was the same nurse that had taken his information when he arrived. She was the boss when the doctor wasn't around, and she let the power go straight to her head. She bent over to get right into the man's face to speak quietly where only the two of them could hear what she was about to tell him. "You're in my world now darlin'. You don't ask questions, and you don't get smart with me. The sooner you get that, the better off you'll be." She stood up slowly and smoothed the creases out of the skirt of her white uniform. "I don't think we can be friends anymore." She looked at the orderlies that had a hold of him under his arms. "Get him out of my sight." She said between her teeth. The orderlies made haste on their orders, and took him to his room. The man understood right then that the Head Nurse was not one he wanted to cross paths with often, because if he did, he might kill her.

CHAPTER 2

The man was awake at 4:43 A.M. He noticed someone had closed the curtains over his window. He laid there awake, staring at the ceiling. He saw the shadow rise in front of the window out of the corner of his eye. The two gleams of red light appeared slowly within the shadow. The man clenched his teeth and kept staring straight ahead, concentrating on the small indents in the ceiling tile. He refused to say a word to it. The shadow softly and incoherently began to whisper out loud to him. The man closed his eyes, and started to breathe heavily trying to drown out the thing whispering by the window.

'They don't care about you, but I do. Just give me what I want.' He heard a voice echo inside his head. He had nothing to make this thing leave him alone. On the outside, he would have gotten high or drunk. All he could do now is concentrate on the sound of his heavy breathing. They finally came to give him breakfast at seven, and he couldn't have been any more relieved. The pretty, softspoken nurse he had met before brought in a plastic tray with a thin slice of ham, hash browns, scrambled eggs, buttered toast, a carton of milk and a container of juice. The moment the lights came on, the shadow disappeared.

"I'm allowed to undo one of your hands for you to eat. Are you right or lefthanded?"

"Left-handed," he replied. She unbuckled the padded strap that held his left hand. She held his head up, and placed an extra pillow behind him. She unwrapped a plastic spoon and napkin, and placed them next to the tray. She opened the juice and the milk carton. The nurse wheeled the bed table over to the man, and she sat in a chair in the corner to wait for him to finish his meal. He noticed that she only spoke when she had too. He couldn't help but wonder if she was a robot programmed to do the basic duties of a nurse.

"When you're finished eating, I'll get your vitals." She said, not even looking up from the chart she had in her hands. He assumed that it was his. He didn't respond to her, because he had a mouthful of food, and didn't really see the point in small talk with anyone here. This was the first time he had eaten since he had gotten to the hospital. The food didn't taste the greatest, but it was sustenance, and he felt half starved. He had the tray emptied and both of the drinks gone in less than five minutes. He belched loudly, and made the nurse look up at him with a look of repugnance. "Well, I'm assuming you're finished." She said flatly.

"Why . . . Whatever gave you that idea?" He said with a cheeky grin. The nurse rolled her eyes, and moved the table away from him. She gathered up the spoon and all the trash, and took it out of the room. She wasn't gone long when she came back in with the blood pressure machine. She had on a pair of blue gloves, and she was removing the electrodes from the back. She took his vitals, and logged it in his chart. She latched his hand back into the strap. She pulled a syringe from her pocket with an alcohol pad. She cleaned a small area on his upper arm and stuck the needle in, and injected some medicine.

"What did you just give me?" The man asked suspiciously.

"Mild sedative. It should kick in by the time the doctor is ready to see you. When it's time to see Dr. Krochek, someone will be back for you. If you are on your best behavior, perhaps you can get out of those restraints, get a shower and join the others in the common room." She gathered the used syringe and trash, and left the room.

Join the others? Who are the others? Crazy people . . . the ones that were screaming outside my door when I first got here. Why would I want to join them? What would we do . . . raise up our crazy flags and start a rebellion?' The thought of this brought a vivid image to his mind. He was leading a bunch of insane, overly medicated and drooling patients in hospital gowns with their bare butts hanging out of the open backs. He was leading them down the corridor. Their flags were made of torn bed sheets, smeared with feces, and drawn on with crayons. They were marching proudly, chanting nonsense. The daydream made him laugh out loud. *'Laughing out loud like that . . . maybe I am one them. Maybe I could be their leader. HA!'* To ignore the darkness that crept in and haunted him, he entertained himself with random thoughts until the head nurse came into his room forty five minutes later. The drugs had kicked in, and made him feel as if he was drunk. That type of feeling always had the man feeling a bit impish. Today she didn't throw open the curtains like she did the day before.

"Are we in a better mood today?" She asked. He could see her trying to hide the sneer when she asked the question. He just gave her a smirk, and turned to stare blankly at the ceiling. "I guess you aren't in a better mood." She added coldly.

"I think it's best I say nothing to you considering everything I want to say to you is . . . how do you put it . . . smart."

"Well, maybe the doctor won't sign off on your restraints."

"Well maybe I should tell your boss you act like Hitler when he isn't around, or maybe I should go to Congress and tell them that you run this place like a prison!" He pulled up on the straps, "lets go honey, I need to see the doctor. Time is of the essence." She glared at him, and roughly let him out of his restraints. "I don't see a wheelchair, I take it I'm allowed to walk today."

"Good luck getting anyone to listen to your mad rants." She mumbled as she helped him sit in an upright position. "We assume you're well enough to walk on your own." She held onto him, squeezing hard, and digging her nails into the flesh of his underarm after she helped him stand. They began the walk to the doctor's office.

"Easy honey, I'm tender." He said, squinting his eyes, and giving her a sideways grin. He knew he was getting under her skin, and he was loving it. The man was already planning on telling the doctor about the nurse, even if she didn't explode on him on the way to his session. "Have you ever thought about becoming a patient here? You seem a little . . . uptight. Maybe the doctor won't sign off on your restraints, but I think you might be into that kind of kink. Are you a freak like that Nurse Satan?" Suddenly, she grabbed him by his shoulders, threw him against the corridor wall, and put her face so close to his that he could smell her pungent breath.

"Listen here, you know nothing about me, and don't even pretend like you do. You don't scare me. You're a nobody. Look at where you are, and look at where I am. Whom do you think the doctor is going to believe? Some delirious sad sack, or a trusted colleague? Why don't you think about that before you run your mouth anymore? I swear that I will make your stay here a living . . . breathing . . . hell."

"Easy does it cheese teeth. Don't get so close to me. I don't want to catch your halitosis." The nurse's face turned deep red with anger. She pressed him against the wall as hard as she could, and her eyes burned into his before she let go of him. They continued their walk, and she swiped her key card violently when they arrived at the double doors. "It's nice to know at least one person in this place will make eye contact and talk to me, even if it's not in a very nice way . . . and their breath is a little . . . corrosive."

"I could have been nice, but you chose to get on my bad side. You don't seem to want to change that."

"It seems like you would rather have everyone on your bad side."

"Don't analyze me, just walk." She let out a sigh of disgust, and jerked at his arm to make him walk faster. "So belligerent." She mumbled under her breath.

They stopped at the fifth door on left. The same intercom and camera system was set up in front of this office. The name on the door read "DR. KROCHEK." The nurse hit the white button on the intercom, and the same buzzing sound was heard on the other side.

"Patient number." A male voice requested from the nurse blandly. The nurse opened the chart, and the camera moved toward them to look at them.

"0043790172."

"Proceed." The door made the same heavy clicking sound as Dr. Montgomery's, and opened. The man and the nurse walked through the door. A tall, lanky man with salt and pepper hair sat behind a large oak desk. The office had the same set up as Dr. Montgomery's office, there was a book case built into the wall, and the same need for new interior design was present. A large machine on wheels with long quarter inch thick, black wires hanging from it sat in the corner behind the desk beside a filing cabinet. In this office, there was no exam table or medical cart, but there was a locked closet in the corner. There were two leather chairs sitting in front of the heavy desk that was similar to Dr. Montgomery's. A woman sat in one of the chairs. At first, the man didn't recognize her. As he got closer, he saw that the woman was his wife. Her blonde hair was pinned up neatly, hiding her curls. She was wearing a black dress that she normally wore to funerals.

"Sandy!" The man said enthusiastically, and he quickened his pace to get beside her. "I knew you would be back for me!" The doctor motioned for him to sit down in the other chair. The man sat on the edge of the chair and reached for his wife's hands. He clasped his hand tightly over hers, but she barely returned the gesture of affection.

"Nurse Adams, please stay. I would like to know what you have observed about his behavior so far." Dr. Krochek ordered dryly. He gave the nurse a look that told her she needed to stay for more serious matters. She took a seat in the corner, and remained silent as she watched what was about to unfold.

"Sandy . . . "The man said quietly. He looked down and saw her tightening her gloved hands into fists around the tissues she held. Doing this released his hands from hers completely. The man was persistent to get through to his wife. "Sandy, it's good to see you. I have missed you sweetheart." Tears began to continuously fall from her brown eyes when he said this. He tried to make eye contact with her, but she would only look down at the tissues in her balled up hands.

"Perhaps now is the best time to tell him, before this has a chance to end badly." Dr. Krochek said quietly.

"Tell me what? What's going to end badly?" There was a painful, long pause. "Tell me what?" The man began to get nervous as time passed slowly with no answers to his questions. "What is it with no one answering me lately?" He pounded the arm of the chair with the side of his one fist. He reached out and rested his hand upon his wife's again. She became tense, but allowed it to happen for the time being. "Sandy . . . our marriage has always been an honest one for the most part. I kept one thing from you, but that was to protect you." He gently rubbed her hand with his thumb. He sighed, and looked down at the floor. "What have you come here to tell me, Sandy?" He pleaded a final time.

"I think . . ." Sandy's voice sputtered. "I know . . . I want a divorce!" She blurted out quickly. She buried her face in tissue of her free hand, and sobbed uncontrollably. The only sound to be heard in the room was her crying. The man was in a state of shock as the word DIVORCE echoed in his mind. No one spoke until Sandy regained her composure. "I'm sorry, Stephan." She said softly, and she removed his hand from hers.

"Sandy, please don't do this." He begged quietly.

"What kind of marriage would we have with you being in here? Am I supposed to stay alone for the rest of my life? How is that fair to me?" She cried, looking at him for the first time since he came into the office. Her makeup was still flawless, even though the tears kept falling.

"Who says I'm going to be in here that long, Sandy?! For crying out loud, have a little hope . . . a little faith! I will get better. Some medication, and I'll be good!" He reached for her hand again, but she dodged his affection by moving away before he could touch her. This made his heart break instantaneously, "please, Sandy! Look at me!" He kept reaching for her, and each time, she moved away from him.

"I'm sorry, Stephan." She whispered, as she pulled her hand away from him again. "Do you need me for anything else? I think I should go now. I need to go." She asked the doctor tearfully. Her voice cracked from whatever turmoil brought on her tears.

"No, you can go." The doctor said gently, as he nodded his head. Sandy wasted no time to stand up, and rush toward the door. Stephan stood up too.

"Sandy! Sandy, please! Stop! Come back, and we can talk about this. Sandy! You know this isn't right!" Sandy didn't turn around, or say another word. "You know what . . . Fuck you too!" His cries fell upon deaf ears. She left the office, and the door slammed behind her. He was left standing there, staring at the closed door inside the room with Dr. Krochek and Nurse Adams. He was trapped inside a nightmare that was truly a reality. He felt his knees buckle, and he collapsed to the floor in front of the leather chair he had been sitting in. He looked at the chair where Sandy had sat, and wished she was still sitting there. He wished he had one more chance to talk her out of her decision to divorce him. The shock of the situation was still setting in when the doctor spoke.

"Please . . . take a seat, and we will have a talk." Dr. Krochek said quietly and calmly.

"What is there left to talk about?" Stephan uttered quietly to the doctor. He was trying to hold it together, but one wrong comment was going to push him passed his limits. He could feel his muscles vibrating from the tension, and it led to him to start shaking slightly. This was visible to the doctor, but Dr. Krochek decided not to say anything. He observed in silence as the sweat began to bead on Stephan's forehead. He watched how his breathing had changed. He watched his muscular chest rise and fall rapidly from the building anxiety.

"Breathe slowly. In . . . two . . . three . . . four . . . and out two . . . three . . . four." Dr. Krochek advised softly. He motioned for Nurse Adams to come to him, and he whispered something to her as he handed her a small key. She went to the locked closet in the corner, and opened it. She retrieved a clean syringe, and a vial of medicine. She measured a dose into the needle and locked the cabinet again. Before Stephan could think twice about it, Nurse Adams had cleaned an area on his arm and injected him with the medicine. "All right, all better now. We have a lot of ground to cover. So, please . . . sit in the chair." Stephan pulled himself off of the floor, and slumped in the chair. He stared at the floor, refusing to make eye contact. He was defeated beyond all measures. He lost his wife, and he was stuck in the hospital. While he was trapped in the hell, he had to deal with the head nurse. "I would like to know how you feel about the situation with your wife." Stephan slowly adjusted his gaze to the doctor, and gave him an unblinking glare of hostility.

"How I feel? You want to know how I feel? You just drugged me AGAIN!" He said through his teeth, "and it feels like someone just ripped open my chest and tore my heart out, and now . . ." Stephan stood up and pounded his fists on the doctor's desk, "NOW . . . YOU WANT TO HANG ME! THAT'S HOW I FEEL. AND YOU HAVE LITTLE MISS HITLER BACK HERE OVERSEEING YOUR WHOLE ENTIRE TORTURE EXPERIMENT! I HAVE BEEN DRUGGED, STRAPPED DOWN, AND RIPPED APART! IS ENOUGH EVER ENOUGH?" He hung his head and clenched his fists tightly. "WHAT THE FUCK ELSE DO YOU WANT ME TO LOSE . . . MY LIFE?" He ran both of his hands through his dark, wavy hair. He wanted to throw something, hit something, cry . . . all at once to feel some relief of what was happening. His world was shattering, and he was helpless to stop it.

"I'm sorry . . . that your wife feels the way she does. No one can make her feel differently. She is right though. What kind of life would she have? Put her best interests first. If you love her . . . then let her be happy." Dr. Krochek said. Stephan fell back into the chair.

"Whose side are you on? I love her enough to get better, that way I can make her happy. Isn't that in your job description . . . to make me better? We've been married for twelve years already. I have known her since the ninth grade.

You don't give up on something like that so easily."

"Well, I think you should know that I'm not recommending a short stay. I want to get a full diagnosis. What we do at our facility is slightly new and experimental. It would require you to stay long term."

"How long are you talking?"

"For me and the staff to do a complete evaluation . . . considering the symptoms given . . . at least six months. That depends on your reaction to our treatment here as well. Some stay for years. But, on another note, Nurse Adams, can you tell me about any negative behavior since the patient's arrival besides his first day."

"Yes, behavior. Yesterday he was given a B52 to calm down, and he had to be put into his bed restraints until today, because he acted out after visiting Dr.

Montgomery."

"That was because I wanted an answer to a simple question, and you weren't giving me an answer. I asked you more than once and you purposely ignored me to set me up to be strapped down again."

"I simply didn't hear you, and you threw yourself on the floor like some kind of . . . maniac." The nurse smiled at him innocently.

"ARE YOU KIDDING ME?" Stephan became outraged all over again.

"Now, Nurse Adams, name calling isn't going to help our cause here. We need to get to the root of the problem here." The doctor said. He looked at Stephan. "Now, have you had a history of such behavior? I recall you were displaying the same difficult behavior when you were first brought to us. Did you ever have problems with such aggression in the past?"

"Who wouldn't fight coming to place like this? Do you think anyone really wants to come here of their own free will? As far as being aggressive toward others in the past . . . not so much. I'm actually a decent guy to get along with.

However, that would've been different if I had met some of you fuck heads on the outside. You're all seriously stupid." Stephan pointed to the nurse and doctor with a malicious glare in his eyes.

"I can assure you that we're not stupid, and our only aim is to help you. You have a valid point about no one wanting to be here, but instead of arguing about this, let's move onto the next thing. I'm going to hook you up to a machine and ask you some questions. The machine will tell if you are being honest or not by measuring your brain waves."

"Okay, so I can't lie my way into sanity and outta this place, huh? Well, maybe you should hook up Nurse Satan over there. Surely, she has some dark secrets that I'm sure you would just love to diagnose."

"Doctor, this man is a nuisance." She interjected.

"This man is here for help, and you are supposed to be a professional!" He reprimanded Nurse Adams. He turned his attention back to Stephan. "Our staff has numerous credentials to work here and no, you most certainly can't lie your way to sanity. Many have tried, and all have failed." He said with an arrogant, thin lipped grin. It was the first smile Stephan saw on the doctor since he entered the room. Dr. Krochek walked over to the machine in the corner behind his desk, and wheeled it over to the chair that Stephan was sitting in. "Nurse Adams, please get his beginning pulse." The nurse obediently did as she was told, and wrote it down in his chart. She assisted the doctor with hooking Stephan up to the machine. It was a series of different wires that were connected to electrodes stuck to the left side of his chest and on eight different spots of his head. He also had to wear a small finger cuff that fit snugly on his pointer finger to measure his pulse throughout the test. A computer tablet was connected to the machine by a USB cord. The doctor stood behind the machine where there was a holographic screen. A picture of Stephan's brain was flashed onto it. It was colored in with a rainbow of colors at first. After a few seconds, the colors settled where they were supposed to be. Stephan's picture of his brain took on a pattern and the doctor observed this. He made some notes on the tablet with a grim look on his face. "I am going to start by asking you some simple yes and no questions, then I will move onto the more pressing yes and no questions. If you lie, this machine is designed to pick up the lie by your brain wave patterns. I will ask you the same question again, and you need to answer honestly. This machine is also designed to catch different patterns of the brain that could help with diagnosing mental health problems. Do you understand?" Dr. Krochek explained to him.

"Yes." Stephan responded. He was already feeling nervous. *'What would the more pressing questions consist of?'* He thought to himself.

"Quite thoughtful already." The doctor said quietly, observing as Stephan's brain pattern and coloring slightly changed. "All right, shall we begin? Is your name Stephan Cranston III?" Dr. Krochek asked.

"Yes." He responded. The doctor made a quick note on the tablet with a stylus before he asked the next question.

"Are you a thirty-six-year-old male?"

"Yes."

"Is the year 2082?"

"No."

"Is the year 2086?"

"Yes." The doctor kept poking at the tablet with every answer.

"Is your birthday April 10, 2050?"

"Yes."

"Is the sky green?"

"No." Stephan responded laughingly.

"All right. We will be moving onto the more serious questions now. Have you often felt irritable or aggressive?" The doctor asked. Sweat began to gradually bead on Stephan's brow. He didn't want to answer any more questions. He felt the urge to rip all the wires off of himself, and run out of the room. He wanted to put this nightmare behind him. He knew how this was going to end, and he knew he needed to go home.

"No." He finally managed to say.

"Again, please answer honestly. Have you often felt irritable or aggressive?" Stephan could feel the heat from the tears beginning to well in his eyes.

"Yes." Again, the doctor made a note.

"Have you felt depressed for no reason?" The overwhelming feeling of defeat washed over him like a tidal wave, but he managed to hold back his tears. He wasn't going to be able to lie, no matter how hard he tried. It would make him look like a sociopath if he tried to lie his way to sanity. He decided the truth was his only option, especially if he wanted a good chance of ever getting out of the hospital.

"Yes." He responded.

"Is there a reason for the depression?"

"No."

"Have you felt on top of the world, accompanied with promiscuity or frivolous spending?"

"No."

"Do you feel like people are out to get you?"

"No . . . yes . . . sometimes."

"Yes or no, please." Dr. Krochek prompted patiently.

"Yes."

"Do you prefer to be alone?"

"No."

"Do you understand written instructions easily?"

"Yes."

"Do you understand verbal instructions easily?"

"Yes."

"Do you feel that you are easily motivated?"

"Yes."

"Have you ever intentionally caused damage to property?" Stephan took a moment before he answered. He didn't like this question, and his answer was worse.

"Yes." He finally said.

"Do you have trouble with the law?"

"No."

"Do you get headaches?"

"Yes."

"Do you experience nausea?"

"Yes." Stephan came to the stunning realization that he had been living with stomach and head aches so long that it was second nature to him.

"Do you have visual or auditory hallucinations without using drugs or alcohol?"

"Yes."

"Do you have irregular sleeping patterns?"

"Yes."

"Do you have nightmares?"

"No."

"Do you have a drug or alcohol dependence?"

"Yes."

"Do you want to hurt or kill anyone else?" Another question Stephan didn't want to answer.

"Yes." He responded quietly. He stared blankly at the floor, knowing that as of now, his life was over.

"Do you have thoughts to hurt or kill yourself?"

"Yes."

"Do you have a plan of how you would do these things?"

"Yes." The doctor finished marking down his last answer.

"I would like to discuss some of your answers a little more in depth. First lets get you disconnected from this machine." Dr. Krochek gestured for the nurse to help. She quickly got up from her seat, and began to remove the electrodes from his head. She ripped at them fast and hard, taking some of Stephan's brown hair out. He grimaced, but wouldn't give her the satisfaction of a yelp. Once the wires were removed, the machine was placed back to its original position behind the doctor's desk. Dr. Krochek took his seat behind he desk with the tablet. Nurse Adams sat next to Stephan, and waited patiently to take him back to the unit.

"Please tell me more about your irritability and aggression. How often do you feel that way?" The doctor inquired.

"You don't wanna keep me hooked up to that machine to make sure I'm not lying?" He rolled his eyes. "Most of the time." Stephan finally replied to the doctor.

"Is there a cause or is it just . . . there?"

"It's just there most of the time. Sometimes things piss me off, but I'm only human. I guess I was born to be a miserable person."

"And the depression, do you feel sad along with those other feelings?"

"Yes, it's because I'm sad that I am irritated, and that pisses me off. Then I get irritated even more, and that bums me out. Then that makes me mad. It's just one vicious cycle that never seems to end. The whole thing causes a great deal of anxiety."

"I see. Your hallucinations, are they visual or auditory?"

"I see and hear . . . something."

"Tell me about that." Dr. Krochek seemed a little too fascinated in this.

"Umm, well . . . I think . . . it's . . . a demon."

"A demon . . . as in . . . from Hell?" The doctor appeared to be dumbfounded, but interested. The nurse looked at him through the corner of her eye, and tried to pretend not to listen.

"Yeah."

"What does it say?"

"It tells me to kill certain people, how I should do it, and why they deserve it. I have been ignoring it since I was twenty-two. I've never hurt anyone . . . ever, I swear. I never told anyone about it either. My wife . . . she caught me talking to it one time. She told me no one was there, and *that's* how I got here. She told me I needed help, and I was just coming to talk to a doctor." Stephan stared with unblinking anger at the floor as he said this. The doctor wrote everything Stephan said in the tablet, and looked at him as he leaned back in his chair.

"Your wife also noticed bouts of depression when you had nothing to be upset about. You seem to have had a pretty good life. A successful business, you were married and had a house. That's also what had her concerned."

"Has she been taking notes? Why are you talking about my life in the past tense? Like it's something, I'm never going to have again." Stephan wondered out loud to himself. He looked at Dr. Krochek, "I'm beginning to think that she put me here, just so she could make it easier on her to divorce me. She was never very fond of confrontation."

"I don't think it's anything like that. I think she's genuinely concerned."

"If she was so concerned, she never would have left me in this God-forsaken place, and then told me she wanted a divorce while I was in here." Stephan said coldly.

"From your answers, it sounds like it's a good thing you're here. The most serious matter is the hallucination, we definitely need to address that.

I'm not saying the other things are not as important." Dr. Krochek said, looking at the machine's results.

"Have you ever thought about hiring different people? It would make this a much better place. Not such a . . . hostile environment." He told him as he looked at Nurse Adams.

"She's one of the best staff we have here. She does what's necessary to keep order on the unit."

"If only you knew . . ." Stephan trailed off.

"Tell me about your sleep patterns." The doctor demanded, ignoring the last remark.

"Sometimes it's hard to sleep, because the demon won't stop talking to me."

"Is it telling you to kill when you're trying to sleep?"

"Yeah, it gets angry because I won't do what it wants."

"Has it told you to hurt or kill anyone close to you?" The doctor sat forward in his chair and rested his forearms on his desk as he asked this.

"Stephan Cranston II, my father. He used to beat on my mom, because she would yell at him for what he did. He was already out of the picture when it started to tell me to kill him."

"What did your father do?"

"I can barely remember the memory. Something about him selling something that he could never get back, and had no right to sell. I know how angry it made my mom, and their marriage suffered for it."

"You never acted on what the demon said?"

"No. No matter what he did to my mom, she still loved him. It would have hurt her to kill him. I couldn't do that . . . not to her."

"Is that the only reason you didn't kill him?"

"I'm not gonna lie . . . she is the only reason he lived as long as he did."

"So, he's gone now . . .?"

"I found out that his heart exploded five years ago. That bastard deserved to die slower."

"Now with him gone, he can't hurt anyone else."

"Yeah I know."

"Where's your mother?"

"She passed away three years ago. So, at least she doesn't have to witness what a shit storm my life has become. I was a happy success as far as she knew when she passed away."

"The drug and alcohol dependence, did you use both or just one before you came here?"

"I drank and smoked pot. It made it go away for a little while. It was nice to have a break sometimes. It helped me sleep when it wouldn't be quiet." The doctor stared at him intently for a moment in silence. Stephan knew what he was thinking from the look in his eyes. Dr. Krochek was thinking that he was crazy enough to never get out of the hospital.

"Did you use marijuana medicinally?"

"It would be considered recreational, because I didn't have a prescription."

"How often did you use alcohol and marijuana?"

"One or the other every chance I got, it was the best way I could remain sane, and live a somewhat normal life."

"Would it be safe to say you used them daily?"

"Yep . . . that would be accurate."

"When you drank, was it beer . . . liquor?"

"Whiskey. When I wanted the voice to stop . . . I made it stop by getting as drunk as possible."

"So the thoughts of hurting and killing someone else . . . that's a demon?"

"Yes, it also tells me how it should be done. If it's not done the right way then it won't work."

"What won't work?"

"Resurrecting Satan." Stephan tried fighting against a smile. "Although, I don't see how any of that is possible when Satan is present in this room with us, right now." Stephan stifled a small laugh.

"How is Satan in this room, and how is it funny?" The doctor asked sternly.

"Don't you see her, Dr. Krochek? Satan is in the form of female Hitler, and she is sitting right beside me!" He couldn't contain himself any longer, and he began laughing hysterically as he pointed to the head nurse. Nurse Adams became red with anger for the second time that day because of him when she realized he was talking about her.

"Dr. Krochek . . . he . . ." The doctor raised his hand, and cut her off from whatever she was about to say.

"Now, that's enough. We have a serious matter on our hands. Let's continue our discussion." There was a small amount of aggravation in the doctor's voice. "What's the reason behind all your sarcasm?" It took Stephan a minute to calm down. When he finally did, he wiped a tear from his eye to give the doctor his answer.

"I don't know, I guess it's just a part of whom I am." The doctor looked at him flatly.

"Hurting or killing yourself . . . please elaborate on that." Dr. Krochek said with a sigh.

"Before, I just thought about hurting myself, but after today and what happened with my wife . . . I want to die. I honestly just don't give a fuck anymore. That heartless bitch is going to take everything from me. I know it . . . my house, my business. Everything that I built, and she is gonna get it while I rot in here. As far plans . . . what could I possibly do in this place? She made sure there would be no consequences for her abandonment. There would be no way of her having to deal with my reaction, or the aftermath. She gets to hire a lawyer to do the dirty work for her too. How much do you want to bet that I don't see Sandy again while I'm here?"

"Usually people hire attorneys in divorce cases. Now, if you weren't in here, and your wife still wanted a divorce, what would your plan be?"

"I would get creative . . . Maybe step out into traffic, and get tossed around like a ping pong ball. Jump over an interstate bridge, and get splattered onto the windshield of a semi. Gun shots to the head are so passe." The doctor's eyes widened a bit, and he made a note in the tablet. "So, doc . . . what's wrong with me? How crazy am I? Most importantly . . . can you shrink me? Isn't that what you're supposed to do?"

"I will go over your diagnosis and medications the next time I see you. No shrinking is involved. I need to write it up. I have one more question for you.

What is your perfect world?"

"My perfect world? What kind of question is that?" Stephan tilted his head to the side, perplexed.

"It's a standard one that we ask everyone here."

"Strange." Stephan murmured. "Well, it's most certainly not here." He told the doctor.

"Well, of course not. Where would it be, and who would be there?"

"Do I have to answer this today? I think this is something I should think about for awhile."

"Absolutely not. Take your time. Sleep on it. I'll see you in a couple of days."

"Do I have to be strapped down any more?" Stephan asked, making sure to receive an answer in front of Nurse Adams.

"No, I don't think you have to be restrained anymore. Unless you prove to have risky behavior, you are free to be in the common room with the other patients. Try thinking about your perfect world before our next visit. In the meantime, I'll be putting your information into this." The doctor slightly raised the tablet to show Stephan. Dr. Krochek dismissed him, and the nurse escorted him out of the office. Once the door shut behind them, and they started walking down the pale corridor, the nurse finally spoke.

"You're going to pay for that little stunt you pulled in there, you know." She said with a low tone, as she gritted her teeth together.

"I figured, but it was *so* worth seeing your face when he berated you." He would hold onto the memory during his stay. It was priceless to him, and he knew he wasn't going to have many more moments like these with the way the doctor was talking. He would visualize what Dr. Krochek did to the nurse every time a situation will have gotten rough because of her. Stephan knew he wasn't going to make things easy for her, and he knew he would see his bed restraints often because of it. It's not like he had a reason to stay out of them, at least that's how he felt. Stephan was always the type to make the best out of a bad situation, so he figured while he was here, he should have a bit of fun.

CHAPTER 3

Stephan casually walked into the common room. It was occupied by three other patients. He noticed a woman with blond, unkempt hair staring through the window with a blank expression. She tapped at her head with her middle finger, and mumbled incoherently to herself. A tall, muscular black man stood in a corner with his back against the rest of the room. His one arm moved wildly in a jerking motion while his other hand rested against the wall. Stephan could only imagine what he was doing. Another woman sat on the end of a vinyl couch with her knees pulled up to her chest with her arms wrapped around them for comfort. Her chin rested on her knees as she stared at the blank screen of an outdated, flat screen television. He noticed she was crying, but still seemed to be the most sane person in the room. He sat on the opposite end of the couch of her.

"Are you as crazy as everyone else in here?" He asked her quietly.

"I don't think so, but they will write it up that way if they want to keep you here." She replied to him, quickly wiping her eyes.

"Is that why you're crying?"

"That, and once you're here . . . you don't leave." She sniffled.

"Yeah, I figured that one out." He mumbled. "What's your diagnosis?"

"Manic depressive, major depression, suicidal thoughts and tendencies, intermittent explosive disorder. I guess I've been crazy all my life, and just never even knew it. What about you?"

"I don't know. I just took the test today." Stephan air quoted the words the test to her.

"Oh, that thing. Don't you love it? I would love to smash that machine. Can't lie your way into sanity." She said mockingly.

"I know. I tried. I swear the whole thing is designed to make everyone look crazy. Maybe Nurse Hitler should take it. She just might end up in here with all of us crazies, and we can give her a good ol' fashioned blanket beating." He said slyly. She let out a small laugh.

"Nurse Hitler?"

"Yeah, you know . . . Adams."

"Oh, why do you call her Hitler?" She asked curiously.

"Let's just say . . . we didn't exactly start off with the best of first impressions."

"She seems a little . . . stern, but she's okay if you stay on her good side."

"Well, I'm definitely not on her good side, and it would seem she set it up to be that way." Stephan explained.

"Are you sure you're not being paranoid?"

"I wish I was . . . maybe then she wouldn't be such a bitch." Stephan sighed.

"Hell, they made me wait like . . . two days to get a shower. It's embarrassing, but I laid in my own piss for half that time."

"Why . . .?"

"I was strapped down."

"Oh, I see. You're that guy. You caused quite an uproar when you got here."

"Oh did I?" Stephan said with sarcastic surprise. "I didn't wanna come here. So, I wasn't going down without a fight."

"Hey, I get it." She threw her hands up. "I should have fought harder when my Aunt dropped me off. I know you don't have a diagnosis, but something brought you here . . . what is it?" Stephan stared at an empty chair in the corner. His lips curled into a toothy smile, and a cloud of darkness rolled over his eyes.

"Over there . . . in that chair . . ." Stephan motioned with his head toward a chair in the corner. "A demon with bright, fiery eyes is sitting in it. It's looking at me, and it's whispering to me. It tells me to kill. It has a name, and it wants me to say it for some reason, but I refuse. I've seen it since I was a young man, but I usually try not to acknowledge it. That pisses it off, and that makes me happy. That's been the only happiness I've had lately. The more I ignore it, the more silent its whispers become. Ignoring it is going to be really hard to do in here though. I can't do the things in here that I was doing on the outside to keep it quiet." He explained to her.

"So, you are crazy too. That's okay. No one is better than anyone else, even though they pretend they are sometimes." She shrugged and slid her feet from the couch.

"Well, maybe it was the bitch I'm soon divorcing, that drove me crazy."

"What do you mean?"

"Heartless. Drops me off, and then waits for my first visit with the doctor to announce she wants a damn divorce. Now, here I sit, waiting to sign away my life when her attorney comes, and there isn't a damn thing I can do about it."

"I'm sorry to hear that. I always say that if they want to leave . . . let them. Some people just are not worth chasing after." Her voice faded, and Stephan thought about how Sandy manipulated him into coming here, and turned his life upside down in a blink. She blind sided him with this decision, and she wasn't answering any of his questions. If anything, she was avoiding him. Stephan realized that the woman he was talking to was right.

"You seem to have some amazing insight when it comes to people." He finally said, breaking the silence between the two of them.

"Why pluck the wings from a butterfly to kill it, when you it's easier to set it free?" The woman said knowledgeably, in a calm voice. He stared at her for a moment and took in what she said to him.

"What's your name?" Stephan asked.

"I'm Rosalie. You can just call me Rosie though." She offered her hand to him.

"I'm Stephan Cranston III. Please don't call me Steph for short." He noticed how soft her skin was against his. She let out a short laugh as they shook hands in their short introduction.

"Well, I bet you think you're quite funny with your lame jokes. You might be good one to have around, especially in a place like this."

"I don't know. I caused quite an uproar in Dr. Krochek's office earlier with Nurse Satan." Rosie tried not to laugh too loud at the nickname for the head nurse.

"If you cause too many problems, they will keep you in restraints you know." She whispered. Rosie looked at him with her bright, green eyes. They were wide, and filled with sadness. Her auburn, unbrushed hair was tied back in a loose ponytail. Stephan looked away. He was already starting to like her. She was nothing like his wife, and he needed a distraction. She seemed more like him, broken and in need of repair. She was insightful, and seemed to have an openmind about the situation because of what life had put her through. Rosie was someone he could talk to while he was stuck in the mess that his wife had stuck him in. Maybe he had found a friend among the filth life was burying him in at that moment.

"So, what's up with everyone else in here?" He asked her, breaking the silence.

"I didn't get anyone's names. I've been skipping out on group sessions. I do know that she is talking back to the voices in her head." Rosie said, pointing to the woman staring out of the window. "He is a chronic masturbator, but at least he is kind enough to do it with his back turned away from everyone." Her commentary made him chuckle.

"This is very true. Kudos to . . . George. His name is George now." Stephan said.

"Okay, he's George." She smiled at him. Stephan noticed she had a pretty smile, and that he liked seeing it instead of her tears. He didn't want to feel this way about her. He looked away quickly and stared at a cracked tile on the floor. *I'm about to get a divorce. I should be grieving. What am I doing? I should be falling apart.'* Stephan scolded himself. Rosie was making him see things from different perspectives, and he didn't know why he liked her so much for it. When he talked to her, he didn't think about his wife or the divorce. He didn't even pay much attention to the fact they were in a hospital. It was as if they were two regular people having a casual conversation on a bench in a park. He couldn't hear the demon, it just cowered in the corner out of sight. Perhaps Rosie was just a rebound. The reason didn't matter to Stephan. She was someone he needed at this time in his life. They talked with each other on the stiff, vinyl couch for what seemed like minutes, but were actually hours. They talked about their lives before the hospital. Everything from where they worked and lived to the mundane. How old they were, and which one had better taste in music and movies. They became silent when they heard the head nurse come into the common room.

"Marcus, quit doing that or you're going to pull it off. Wanda, you're going to tap a hole in your skull if you keep doing that." She said as she rolled her eyes." All patients need to be back in their rooms. Anyone who gives me a problem will be dealt with accordingly." She looked at Stephan as she said this and adjusted her collar. He and Rosie got up from the couch and exited the common room. They walked slowly down the hallway together.

"We can talk later." She told him. Rosie tapped Stephan lightly in the arm with the back of her hand while giving him a small half smile. "This is my room."

"What do you know . . . we're across the street from each other." Stephan said with a grin. "Quick, gimme your address, and I'll send you a post card."

"Darn, I can't make it to the post office to pick up my mail." She made it to her doorway and pointed to the small window. "Do you know sign language?" Rosie asked jokingly.

"I know this one." He stuck up his middle finger. She put her hand over her mouth to keep from making any noise. She and Stephan were acting like teenagers.

"You better not get me in trouble." She scolded Stephan.

"I would never do that." He said quietly as he smoothly swept his way into his room. "So, what are we supposed to do?"

"Nothing. A lot of . . . nothing." She sighed as she rested her head against her doorway.

"We can't even read a book?" He asked, aghast.

"No. We can't have anything in our rooms. They're afraid we might find a way to turn it into a weapon." She told him as she rolled her eyes.

"Great . . . can't wait for this to happen. At least George has something to do . . ." He leaned his back against his doorway. The sound of heels clicking rapidly on the tiles could be heard.

"In your rooms!" Nurse Adams yelled as she chased Wanda and Marcus down the hallway, and into their designated rooms. Stephan and Rosie stepped away from their doorways, and the nurse made sure the doors closed behind them.

In his room, Stephan had nothing to do, but stare out of his window to ignore the shadow in the corner. He hummed quietly to himself to drown out the whispers that kept getting louder by the day. He still refused to acknowledge its presence. The sun was shining brightly and he wished he could feel it on his face. He watched an orderly walk the grounds with a patient while they smoked a cigarette. If he had known he would end up in a place like this, he would have taken up smoking cigarettes. Maybe then, they would let him outside. He observed a faded, green truck coming from behind the building and down the driveway going towards town.

An hour passed, and his door opened. A brunette nurse poked her head in, "line up for lunch in ten minutes." She closed the door instantly. Stephan could feel his excitement rising inside himself. He could see Rosie again. Maybe he would sit and eat lunch with her. He wondered if they would be allowed in the common room after lunch. He wanted to sit and talk with Rosie more. She made this place much more bearable, and he found himself wanting to be around her as much as possible. Finally, the ten minutes passed and the patients' doors were opened. They were ordered to line up in a single filed manner. The patients were led to a large room with round tables that had four plastic chairs around each one. There was a full service buffet at one side of the room. A woman with a hair net stood behind it, waiting for the patients to approach. Behind the sixty-seven-yearold disgruntled service woman was a large doorway that led to the kitchen. The line went to a buffet bar. Each patient grabbed a plastic tray and a set of wrapped cutlery with a napkin. Their options were ham sandwiches or sloppy joes with a salad and mashed potatoes. There was a runny looking pie for dessert. There were individual juice boxes to drink along with milk or decaffeinated coffee. Stephan inconspicuously looked for Rosie. He spotted her second from the end of the line. He stood fifth from the end. He received his tray, and made his way over to the coffee machine. He didn't drink coffee, but he figured it was a good way to stall to let her catch up to him. His plan worked as he had planned. Rosie strolled up beside him and playfully bumped into his shoulder. Black coffee spilled over the brim of the biodegradable cup.

"Hey newbie, the coffee here sucks." She said, trying to be helpful.

"That's okay. I'm not much of a coffee drinker." Stephan replied.

"Why are you getting it then?"

"It's here . . . and I like to live dangerously." He said with a smile, "so, where are we sitting?"

"We . . . what makes you think I want to sit with you?" She said smiling. They chose a table in the corner of the cafeteria where it was most likely no one else would sit with them.

"Where did all these other patients come from? I don't see them on the unit." Stephan asked.

"There is a short stay unit for people whose symptoms are less severe. They don't qualify for what they do on our unit." Rosie explained.

"That's such bull shit! A short stay unit? What do you mean they don't qualify? Qualify for what?" Rosie was silent as she slowly chewed her food.

"You don't know about the experiment here?" She asked in between bites.

"Dr. Krochek briefly mentioned something experimental."

"Were you asked about your perfect world yet?"

"Yes! And it's a strange question to be asked in a place like this."

"Yeah, well. They eventually give you that world . . . long story short. I can't really explain it any better, because I've never experienced it." Stephan still had questions that she couldn't answer. For the rest of lunch, they engaged in small talk while they both ate greasy sloppy joes, runny mashed potatoes smothered in lumpy gravy, and salads that had lettuce turning brown drenched in cheap ranch dressing. He learned that they would be forced to have an hour of "Quiet Time" after lunch. In reality, it was for the shift change to go smoother. After that, they would be allowed in the common room for free time until group therapy started. Stephan liked the idea of group therapy. That would be his chance to have a bit more fun. He found himself excited by the idea that Nurse Tracy Adams helped run the group.

During quiet time, Stephan stared out of his window again. He watched the same green truck from before pull in, and disappear behind the building. He found himself wondering where it went, and whom it was driving. Time slowly passed, but before he knew it, Stephan was sitting on the same stiff couch next to Rosie.

This time she sat in the middle of the couch and they were chatting quietly. Stephan was also observing the new patients in the room. A woman he never saw before was sitting in a wheelchair. Long strands of her disheveled gray hair hung in her face. Thick, slimy drool escaped from the one side of her cracked lips. It dripped slowly to her leg and was absorbed by her hospital gown. She had a glazed look in her pale, blue eyes, and she moved in slow motion. Marcus was in his usual corner, vigorously tugging on himself. Wanda was looking through the same window she always did, tapping on her head with her finger. A middle-aged man with his mouth twisted in a permanent scowl sat in the corner by himself. He ran one of his fingers up and down his left arm, as if to motion if he had the means, he would slit open his wrist. Nurse Adams walked into the room with another female patient, and set her down in the chair that was adjacent to the couch. Without saying a word, she briskly turned and walked out.

"Hello." Rosie said to the woman. The patient responded by nervously twitching her fingers on the side of her leg, and her head jerked downward suddenly.

"The fucking bitch is a filthy asshole!" She said loudly as her head violently jerked forward. She nervously smacked her leg as hard as she could.

Stephan couldn't contain himself and he bursted out with laughter.

"That's right, sister. You tell it how it is!" He finally managed to say, wiping tears from his eyes.

"That is enough!" Nurse Adams walked in with a short, balding man wearing wire framed glasses. He was holding a small stack of papers, and his name tag read THERAPIST. In other words, another one of Nurse Adam's dancing monkeys. "Marcus, Wanda, please come over and join us." She asked as she turned the drooling, wheelchair-bound woman toward the sitting therapist. Marcus still had his one hand under his hospital gown as he made his way over to a chair furthest away from everyone else in the group, and didn't allow his hand to stop. Wanda still kept looking out of the window as if she didn't hear the nurse. Nurse Adams had to physically direct her to join the group. Even sitting, she still tapped on her head and mumbled to the voices in her head as she rocked back and forth rapidly.

"Is everyone here?" The therapist asked Nurse Adams.

"Yes, these are all we have that aren't put under." She responded, keeping the conversation between just the two of them. She looked around the group, and then gave the fake, cheesy smile that she first gave Stephan when he first saw her.

"Okay, since we have some new faces, how about we start with some introductions. I'll go first. I'm Nurse Adams." She spoke to the group like she was addressing a kindergarten class. She motioned to the therapist to go next.

"I am your therapist who assists Nurse Adams with the group therapy sessions. Everyone knows me as Mr. S."

"That's good. Now we have Wanda . . . hi Wanda." Nurse Adams tried to get the attention of the patient poking her own head.

"They said you . . . is a bitch . . . and not worth talking too." Wanda said as held up one finger at the nurse. She never made eye contact and went back to mumbling and tapping. Stephan scoffed loudly, and this made Nurse Adams shoot him a look of contempt.

"Okay then . . . Paul, would you like to pull your chair closer to the group?"

She asked the brooding man sitting in the corner.

"What's the point? No one can take it away. You can't help me. There is only one thing left to do, and you only want to stop it." He never looked up, but just kept tracing an invisible line up and down his arm. Stephan began to wonder why Wanda and Paul didn't get the whistle blown on them or get the same Nurse Adams he would get if he had answered that way.

"Rosalie, you're looking well today." Nurse Adams said.

"Thanks." Rosie responded nodding her head, but avoiding eye contact.

"Marcus, I do wish you would stop doing that long enough for us to have a group."

"And I wish . . . you would get off . . . my case. We don't . . . always get . . . what we want though." He told Nurse Adams between slow strokes. She looked away from him, and went about conducting the group. She looked at the woman sitting in the wheelchair.

"Everyone who remembers Mabel, she will be proceeding to one of the Control Rooms today. Until then, let's make her feel like she is part of the group." Nurse Adams gave Mabel a thin lipped grin. Mabel tried to smile back, but only managed to let a large glob of drool escape down her chin. "Lily, I always love to hear what you have to say." She said, turning to the nervous, twitching woman sitting next to the couch.

"A fucking bitch is a filthy asshole!" She yelled as she did before while jerking her head downward. Stephan bit onto his fist to keep himself from laughing, but he still caught the attention of Nurse Adams.

"Ah yes, Stephan . . . how could I . . ."

"Please, I can introduce myself." He said, cutting her off. He stood up, and puffed out his chest. "I am Sarcastic Stephan, and I am here to redo the introductions. They weren't done very well the first time, I'm afraid." He said looking at Nurse Adams, and clasping his hands together. "Let me start with you Wanda . . . Wandering Wanda. Those voices are steering you in the right direction dear, but don't you get a headache at the end of the day with all that tapping? You must have a soft spot there by now."

"They told me . . . you were an asshole." Wanda hissed.

"They're probably right." He averted his attention to the woman in the wheelchair. "Mabel . . . Mushy Marbles Mabel. I call you this, because that's all that is left of your brain sweetheart. That's not your fault though, I'm sure it's because these savages are over medicating you, deary. Marcus . . . Masturbating Marcus, I call you George behind your back, so you could also be . . . Genitals George. I say you should go for the gold. It's your dick, you play with it all you want, buddy."

"Fuck you prick!" He responded abruptly.

"Hey, I'm on your side pal." Stephan turned to direct his attention to the man sitting away from the group. "Paul . . . Purposeful Paul . . ."

"What the fuck do you want, asshole?" He stopped tracing the invisible line up and down his arm, and glared at Stephan.

"I admire your determination to end your life, but what the hell do you have to be depressed and suicidal about that brought you here? Is life really that horrible for you? Have you ever considered closing your suicide lane, and maybe . . . just maybe opening a detour in another direction?"

Stephan made a sideways slicing motion across his wrist. "Won't kill you, but it will still make you feel great!"

"You don't know me ass hat, so shut the hell up." Paul looked down at his arm again, and proceeded to trace his line of comfort up and down his arm.

"Well, okay. I guess I'll let hostility win this one. I think Lily says what we are all thinking. Am I right Loudmouth Lily?" He looked at the nervous, twitching woman sitting in the chair.

"F . . . f . . . fucking asshole!" Her head violently jerked downward and her fingers started twitching against her leg. "A filthy bitch!"

"I completely agree." Stephan closed his eyes and nodded his head. He placed his fingers together like a steeple in a sign of superiority and raised them to his chin.

"Rosie . . . Ravishing Rosie. I have nothing but good things to say about you. You make my stay here so much better. Considering everyone here, you are one of the sane ones." This comment made Rosie deeply blush, and she put her hand up to her face to hide her smile. Stephan turned to the therapist, and waved at him with his right hand. "Mr. S, you're just a letter and I . . . am just a number. So, really you're just a patient that gets to go home at the end of the day." He looked at Nurse Adams, and his sarcasm faded and was replaced with the wicked truth. "I saved the best for last . . . or should I say worst. Nurse Satan . . ."

"I think we all have heard enough of your little rant." Nurse Adams finally interrupted.

"I think we should let him express his feelings, even if they are negative. It's very therapeutic." Mr. S said quietly to her.

"You see. You don't know everything. The people haven't heard enough, and you're just the tyrant that thinks you know everything and doesn't want to hear another person's opinion." Stephan said bitterly.

"You must really feel at home in those restraints." Nurse Adams said as an evil smile slightly emerged across her face.

"You must really hate your job since you're not afraid to lose it!" He replied, being as combative as possible. "I'm really sure that everyone here would agree with me that you're a fussy bitch that should be admitted here as a patient to face some of your own deep-rooted issues. Maybe they wouldn't agree, because it seems like I'm the only one you like to shit on.

Genitals George here pretty much told you to go fuck yourself, and you didn't even flinch." Stephan stepped behind Mabel's wheelchair and rested his hands gently on her shoulders. He bent over so he could speak quietly to her. "What do you have to say about all this mush'ems?" He whispered in her ear. He stood up abruptly, and threw his hands out to his side as he shrugged his shoulders. "Nothing . . . nothing at all, because she is so out of it. These dictators who call themselves medical professionals . . . are a joke. Nurse Hitler over here does it all with a smile on her face. Here's my diagnosis for you, bitch." He said as he strolled over to Nurse Adams. "Psychopathic sadist with signs of being a serial killer. I believe the shoe fits so lace it up tight and wear it proudly, because people like you don't change. Oh, one more thing. For the love of GOD . . . buy a toothbrush and use the damn thing! Your breath is like mustard gas! Which is funny being that you're female Hitler! This couldn't get any better!"

Those last words were like hands grabbing the head nurse around the throat and squeezing like a constrictor. Never in her time of working there, had a patient gotten up the nerve to talk to her that way. She stood up abruptly and glared at Stephan.

"Do you think you're being funny?" She yelled.

"I think I'm funnier than a pro-life vegetarian eating a fucking scrambled egg!" Stephan screamed back. The nurse pulled at the thick chain holding her whistle, and blew on it. The obedient orderlies briskly walked into the room before Stephan could get another word out. He decided that he was going to put up a fight against them this time, but he was no match for them. They effortlessly had him on his belly and had him restrained. He knew he wasn't going to be able to take them, but he had fun trying. He kicked, laughed and shrieked like a mad man. "We all end up like Mabel because of these Nazis! Everything I said was worth this shit!" He screamed and laughed maniacally as he was carried out of the common room. "I think this group was very productive! You've all been a lovely audience!" He called back enthusiastically, still shrieking like mad man down the hall to his room.

"Group therapy is over for today." Nurse Adams said as calmly as she could with a quiet, shaky voice. She stood up and left the common room quickly, taking Mabel with her. Mr. S gathered his papers, and was right behind her with Lily.

"Did that shit seriously just happen?" Paul said quietly from his corner, with a creeping smile on his face. He pushed his black hair to the side, revealing his chiseled features, and vibrant blue eyes that were filled with excitement from the events that had just happened.

"Yes. Yes it did." Rosie said, still in shock from the experience. She let out a sigh and just shook her head. There was nothing else to do since Stephan would be strapped down again.

CHAPTER 4

Stephan was in his restraints overnight and into the afternoon of the next day. In the night, he slept deeply and had a strange dream. He was a small boy again, and he was with his father in the old red truck they had when he was a child. They were driving on a highway that was vaguely familiar to him, and he couldn't figure out why. In the dream, his father took him to a large, stone building that looked like an old chapel. He held Stephan's small hand as he led him inside the structure. He felt scared and didn't want to go in the building. His father had to start practically dragging him the closer they got to their destination inside. Waiting at an altar at the front of the building, were people in long, black robes. Then everything tunneled into black emptiness, and he saw the dark shadow with the red eyes. It engulfed him, and seemed to overtake who he was as a person. The being began to scream at him. The wailing was so loud and deafening, that Stephan held his hands to his ears. He started to scream back at it and was awakened by a nurse bringing him a tray for breakfast.

"Must have been some dream you were having . . . you were screaming in your sleep." She told Stephan, without an ounce of concern in her voice. He didn't say anything back to her. He realized he was sweating and crying, but decided not to dwell on the dream too much. He figured it was the demon trying to mess with him since he was ignoring it. If his crazy couldn't attack him when he was awake, it would try to get him through his sub conscious.

Yet again, only one hand could be undone for him to eat. This time he was at peace with it because of how peeved Stephan knew he had left Nurse Adams after the group therapy session the day before. It was easy to ignore the red-eyed demon, and its growing whispers when he was awake. He had the vision of her red face and the pulsating vein in her forehead. All it would've taken was for someone to poke at it for it to explode. How the therapist reminded the nurse of what was therapeutic. These images danced in his head and brought him immense joy. The memory helped to pass the time while he lie in his bed after he finished his breakfast and the nurse left. Before he knew it, Nurse Adams was in his room to take him to see the psychiatrist. They walked in silence and were at the double doors when she finally spoke. "You weren't scheduled to see the doctor until tomorrow, but I'm sure it's your stunt yesterday that has him anxious to see you. I'm going to tell you something right now, if you plan to act foolish in this session like you did the other one . . . your goose will be cooked as far as I'm concerned."

"Yessa Massa!" Stephan said sarcastically. The grip she had on his arm tightened to let him know to quit what he was doing immediately and that she was serious. He chuckled quietly to himself the whole way down the corridor. They approached Dr. Krochek's door, and went through the same routine as they did before with the intercom and camera. They stepped inside the office. When the doctor saw the annoyed look on Nurse Adams' face, he asked her to stay out of concern for her. Stephan took his usual seat on the right facing the desk . . . the opposite chair that his wife sat in when she announced she wanted a divorce.

"Well, what do we have to say today as far as the patient's behavior from yesterday, Nurse Adams?" Dr. Krochek asked her as she sat down. He had an electronic tablet in his hands with a stylus to begin taking notes. Stephan's paper chart sat on the desk.

"He made a horrid display in the group therapy session yesterday. He made fun of other patients and staff members, myself included. He had a very foul mouth and fought against the orderlies when the time came to be restrained. He acted like . . . like . . . a miscreant!" Nurse Adams sounded like she was pouting about the situation.

"No need to get emotional. We need to assist this man. Group therapy is supposed to be a safe place where he can express himself." The doctor told her.

"You sound like Stevens . . ." Her voice trailed off as she rolled her eyes and crossed her arms.

"I asked to see you a day early because of your diagnosis." Dr. Krochek said to Stephan.

"Really! According to her you were anxious to talk to me about my behavior yesterday." He said, motioning toward Nurse Adams.

"No, we addressed that. We need to start you on medication right away. I have written you up as a major depressive because of your chronic sadness. Do you have any questions about this?"

"Am I like Paul? Because that guy . . . needs a bit more meds for depression than me. You really shouldn't waste that diagnosis on me." Stephan said argumentatively.

"I can't discuss other patients with you. More than one person can be depressed, and there are different ways of being depressed. Your depression can be different then another person's. You can't define your diagnosis by someone else's.

"Okay then. So I'm depressed. Now that we know this, doc. How do we fix it?"

"We will talk medications after I go over your diagnosis with you. There is a strong possibility of intermittent explosive disorder, because of your irritability and aggression, and the fact that you act on it. Do you have any questions about this?" The doctor looked up from the tablet.

"I wouldn't say I really acted on it when I wasn't in here. I didn't get into fist fights or anything like that." Stephan protested as he sat forward. He rested his forearms on his thighs, and ran his fingers through his hair. He let out a sigh of frustration as he stared at a small tear in the carpet.

"No, but according to your wife . . ."

"Soon to be ex-wife. Let's not forget this place has done nothing but ruin my life." Stephan interrupted, slumping back into the chair with a thud. He drew the attention of the doctor, and he looked up from the tablet.

"Okay, according to your soon to be ex-wife, you did have fits of rage. Screaming over the simplest of things, slamming doors, and breaking things when you were angry."

"Fine, I guess I could've handled my anger a little bit better than I did. A bit late for any of that. The bitch left me here to rot, now didn't she?" Stephan said with a malicious tone.

"She didn't leave you here to rot . . . she's just moving on with her life, and it just so happens that it doesn't include you." The doctor said impetuously, looking at the tablet again. Stephan was getting on his nerves by interrupting him and giving him sarcastic remarks.

"The auditory and visual hallucinations show that you are schizophrenic with paranoid delusions. This also seems to be causing a state of insomnia along with suicidal and homicidal tendencies. Do you have any questions?" Dr.

Krochek looked up from the tablet again and made eye contact with Stephan.

"I never acted on the homicidal and suicidal shit. They were just thoughts . . . because of the voice stuff."

"We write it up as that, because there is a chance of you acting on it." The doctor put the tablet and stylus down on his desk, and looked intently at Stephan. "The next thing I'm about to tell you . . . may be difficult to hear."

"Yeah, because everything in this place so far has been a walk in the park, let me tell ya." Stephan scoffed. The doctor sighed, but remained calm.

"The machine picked up a pattern on your brain that is only found in a certain class of people, Stephan." Dr. Krochek reached for the paper chart on the desk and brought out three pictures. He hung them on a white screen, flipped a switch and a light turned on. "The brain on the right is a normal brain. The middle brain is your brain, and the left brain is . . ." The doctor paused. He appeared to be a bit nervous.

"What is it, doc? What's wrong with that brain, because it looks just like mine?"

"That pattern is commonly found in serial killers." The doctor finally said. He turned off the light, and quickly ripped the pictures down.

"Well, I guess I'm never getting out of here then, huh?" He asked Dr.

Krochek. "Looks like you have your reason to keep me here for awhile."

"I . . . can't really give you that answer right now." The doctor appeared to be nervous around Stephan now that he knew how mentally ill he actually was.

"I'm completely bat shit crazy, just say it."

"If that's how you want to put it . . . I would say you are a man in need of some help." The doctor responded awkwardly.

"I guess you better give me something really good doc."

"Medication you mean?"

"Well . . . personally, I was hoping you were going to let me fish bowl a fat ounce of reefer, while sipping some whiskey in my own little corner of the universe." Stephan smiled. The doctor sighed with great disdain, and chose to disregard the remark. He picked the tablet and stylus back up from the desk.

"I would like to start you on a fairly old medication for your schizophrenia called Thorazine. We have had great results with it over the decades, and I think it would be a good fit for you. I think starting you on a lower dose . . . lets say twenty five milligrams would be beneficial to start. I'm also going to put you on ten milligrams of an anti anxiety medicine called Buspar. I think putting you on seventy-five milligrams of Wellbutrin for your depression would be beneficial as well. Let's see how you do with those three medications for now, and I'll check on you in a couple days, and we will go from there." Dr. Krochek poked at Stephan's tablet, and looked at him. "Have you given any more thought to what your perfect world would be if given that choice?" He asked.

"Yes. I do know what it would be and I must say, you might disagree." Stephan said in low voice. "Before I tell you though, could she leave the room? I'm a little uncomfortable with her knowing such intimate details about me." The doctor looked at Nurse Adams and motioned for her to wait outside his office door. She was hesitant to leave, but obeyed her boss. Stephan kept his satisfaction to himself when she left in a huff. When the door closed behind her, Stephan looked at Dr. Krochek. "Where do I begin?" He said with seriousness that the doctor had never seen before. "The one who was supposed to stand by me until death bailed on me in my time of need, and kind of got me into the shitty situation I'm in right now. There is a light at the end of this dark tunnel though, and her name is Rosalie. I think she could be my perfect world."

"It wouldn't be having your wife back?" The doctor was stunned with what Stephan said.

"You know, I thought it would be until I met Rosie. I just see so much of myself in her. She is so different from Sandy . . . and that's what I find most appealing about her. My wife should have stuck by me through this. For better or for worse . . . in sickness and in health. It meant nothing to her. She abandoned me, so fuck her. I don't want my wife. She doesn't want me. Even if I could have it my way, I'm not going to force someone to be with me."

"What if in this world, you wouldn't remember being here or your wife dropping you off? Everything could be as it was. Your wife would be happy. You would have your house and business. You wouldn't be forcing her to be with you." Stephan paused for a moment and gave this a thought.

"I know what I know now though. Sandy shattered my heart and my whole world. She wants a fabulous new life without me . . . so if given the chance . . . I would live on without her too." Stephan's voice broke a little as he held back tears.

"I recall you saying that you weren't going to give up on her very easily. What happened to that man?" Dr. Krochek asked inquisitively.

"What happened to the woman who was supposed to stand by me in sickness and in health . . . for better or worse? It was all bull shit to her. The vows we made in front of God . . . meant nothing to her. If they did, she would never have done this to me."

"Well, being that Rosalie is a patient . . . it is rather disagreeable and unorthodox, but it's possible. It's never been done before, but if that's your request . . . so be it." Dr. Krochek replied.

"Yeah, and from what I understand . . . your experiment is unorthodox. So, just give me what I want without your commentary." Stephan said snidely. "I also want to be respected, with a good job that suits me better than selling furniture. I would want a beautiful home with a garden. My dream car . . . a black, twentieth century '69 Dodge Charger, with a 440 fuel-injected engine." Stephan paused and closed his eyes as he imagined the car. He bit his lip and he smiled. He came out of the fantasy, and set his attention on the doctor. "What is all this for anyhow? Why are you asking me this?" Stephan asked inquisitively. He recalled what he and Rosie talked about before. This was the time to ask the questions she couldn't answer for him.

"I'm sure you have had the pleasure of meeting our . . . Mabel since your arrival."

"Yeah, I met Mushy Mabel." Stephan said with a laughing sigh.

"Quite the nickname, but anyway. Every patient will eventually come to know the same process as she has, then they can be put into a nocturnal state. This way they can be introduced to their perfect world through virtual reality machines. It's almost like a semi-permanent dream. You will remain sedated, and live happily in your perfect world for as long as deemed necessary." The doctor explained the whole process to him very bluntly. Stephen was too shocked to say anything at first.

"And . . . how long will you deem it necessary for me to be in your experiment, doc?"

"I can't answer that question right now. It all depends on how well you respond to the treatment." Dr. Krochek responded.

"So you do this to everyone that comes through this place?"

"Only the patients that meet the requirements. It's no mystery. We have made our purpose here very open to the public. In fact, there have been medical journals written up on what we do. We have taken the next step into psychiatric care. Now that I know your perfect world, your process can begin." He held a button on a small box on his desk and spoke to the nurse in the hallway. "Please take the patient back to the unit. We are finished here."

"So . . . why can't you just put me on some meds, and send me on my way back into the real world? Isn't that what you should be *really* doing in here? It's a much more noble and ethical goal."

"We always see the same people back in here in three to six month having another nervous breakdown, or you forgot to take your medications. This way no one has to worry. Murders have decreased significantly since we started doing this with the mentally ill. Diagnose someone as a sociopath, and they are put under for the rest of their lives." Dr. Krochek was very matter of fact about it all. Stephan wanted to drop his jaw, but refused to give the doctor any satisfaction of shock value.

"So how long will you deem it necessary for me to be put under?" Stephan asked the doctor again. "I know you have the answer to that, you're just avoiding giving me the answer. I can see through your bull shit, doc."

"Like I said before, that all depends on how you respond to the treatment."

Dr. Krochek said very methodically. It was as if he had said this same line a hundred times before, and would say it a thousand times more.

"It's going to be forever because of what you said about my brain pattern. I just know it." He mumbled to himself so the doctor wouldn't hear him. Stephan waited for the head nurse to be back in the office before he asked his last question.

"Am I allowed out of my restraints, doc?"

"I don't see the harm as long as you don't cause any more problems in group therapy sessions."

"I'll try not to." Stephan replied.

"Don't try . . . just do." The doctor ordered, not looking up at them. He was too busy transferring Stephan's paper chart to the electronic tablet. Nurse Adams held him tightly by the arm, and led him out of the office towards the patient's unit in silence. She had nothing to say to the most willful patient she ever had in her history of employment at Euphoria Hills Institution. She had been pushed to her limits before, but never beyond them. When he was back on the unit, he made his way back to the common room, hoping to see Rosie. When he got there, he saw Wanda, Marcus and Paul, but no Rosie. Stephan decided to sit on the couch, and wait for her. Wanda was doing her usual tapping and mumbling, and Marcus was doing his daily routine in his corner. A voice from the corner caught Stephan's attention.

"Hmm, they let you out of your cage I see." Paul said sharply. Stephan looked over, and he saw he was sitting in his usual chair in the corner. In the seat next to him, sat the demon with the glowing red eyes. It quietly whispered to him, turned its head sideways and hissed at Stephan. He quickly put his attention on Paul.

"Yes, they tend to do that on account of good behavior." Stephan responded with a wide grin. "I'm surprised you feel you're not better than the rest of us and not hiding away in some corner by yourself."

"What's that supposed to mean?" Paul asked arrogantly.

"Aren't you some kind of depressed, suicidal, narcissistic, lunatic? Why would you want to lurk in here with the manics and schizos? Aren't you better than the rest of us crazies?" Stephan made a circular motion along the side of his head with his pointer finger.

"Fuck you. I didn't know asshole was an emotional disorder." Paul shifted in his chair to turn his body away from Stephan as much as he could without moving to another chair.

"It isn't, but I guess not handling constructive criticism is, because that's what you have a lot of you little emo prick."

"I'm not emo. I would do it the right way to actually bleed out and die, thank you very much." Paul sighed, and rolled his eyes.

"Oh I see! That makes you *so* much cooler!" Stephan cackled.

"You don't even know why I'm here, or anything about me."

"Well, why don't you enlighten me so I won't be such an asshole, and hurt your poor, suicidal feelings anymore."

"Telling someone like you anything would be a waste of time. You come off as a very self centered person that has no understanding for human emotion."

"I have plenty of understanding for emotions, if you're a person worth my time. Paul . . . are you someone worth my time?"

"Why would I want your validation?"

"It wouldn't be validation . . . I just want an explanation as to why your life isn't worth living. What brought you here Paulie?"

"I don't think I have to explain that to you." Paul hissed. He started digging his nails into his arm. Stephan noticed a fairly fresh scar along the major vein in his arm. The line Paul traced wasn't so invisible after all. He dug his nails harder into the scar, and it began to seep blood. Paul's eyes grew wide and lively, and a smile crept across his face at the sight of what he had done to himself.

"According to Nurse Satan . . . we're all friends in here." Stephan said in a more hushed tone as he watched Paul mutilate himself, and get pure enjoyment from it.

"I'm not friends with anyone in here. I didn't want friends outside of here. I'm happy with being pathetic and alone." Paul kept his attention on the small trickle of blood he managed to express from the scar on his arm.

"Okay . . . good luck with that you fucking weirdo." Stephan mumbled and the moment he said that, Rosie walked into the common room. She sat on the couch next to him. "You just missed my battle royale with that guy." He said to her as he pointed to Paul.

"Wish I could've seen it, but I was with Dr. Wagner. I told her my perfect world today." She said.

"I did that too with Dr. Krochek. What's your ideal place?" He asked her.

"You first, I'm a little embarrassed of mine."

"No, I asked you first, so it's only fair . . ." Stephan said almost taunting her.

"Promise me that you won't laugh."

"I promise. Cross my heart." Stephan traced an invisible X over his heart.

"Okay, my idea of a perfect world . . . is to be a lesbian porn star." Rosie whispered with a straight face.

"Wow. Th . . . that's really . . . hot!" Stephan finally managed to stammer.

"I might have to join Genitals George in a quick weiner waltz." Rosie laughed hard, and they both heard Paul grumble as he got up and left the room.

"Your turn."

"I don't know if mine would top being a lesbian porn star. Maybe I'll just keep it to myself." Stephan turned red and sank back into the couch.

"Well, that's just not right!" Rosie exclaimed. "Come on big man. I showed you my goods, now you gotta show me yours." She pushed him lightly in the arm. He hesitated at first, but the look in her eyes told him she wasn't going to give up until she knew. He sighed, and leaned in close to her to whisper in her ear.

"My perfect world . . . is you." He inched away slowly. He stared at her and waited for her reaction. He could feel himself turning redder by the second.

"That's good to know." She looked at him and smiled. Her green eyes were filled with happiness. "Mine is still being a lesbian porn star." She waited a second, and finally gave a small laugh. "Come on, you're an idiot if you don't think I told Wagner to make my world with you."

"Seriously?" He asked. "You had me going for a minute."

"Yeah . . . I wasn't sure if I should have told you." She said nervously. "You have a wife still technically." She started to pick at her nails to avoid his gaze. "I had no way of knowing if you felt the same way about me. We never went passed the friends stage. You never let on if you liked me that way."

"My wife is divorcing me. She told me at my first visit with Dr. Krochek. At that moment I wanted to die. I thought I had nothing left, but then I met you and everything . . . everything was different. All I know is there is something here. All I want to do is kiss and hold you. I know I can't do either of those things and it sucks. There is definitely something here between us, because when I'm with you, it's almost as if we're not in this place. My wife didn't bend me over and . . . well, you know." He made a derogatory motion with his hand and fist.

"I know. It's worse knowing you're right across the hall from me. Maybe this was supposed to happen though. We had to come to this hell hole to meet each other, and for you to see the true colors of your wife." Rosie explained.

"Lesbian porn star. That was definitely creative. How did you know I would like that one?"

"Because you are a guy, and guys almost always think with that head in their pants instead of the one on their shoulders . . . no offense, but look at Genitals George. He is a prime example of what I'm talking about."

"He gives the rest of us men a bad name. Not all men are like that you know."

"You liked the lesbian comment . . . so." She smiled as she said this, because she knew she had him, and she was right. He fumbled for something to say, but he had nothing. For once, Stephan was speechless.

"So, what's your world with me like?" Stephan said, changing the subject. Rosie giggled knowing that she made him flustered.

"Umm . . . a house . . . that I would take care of while you went to work. Maybe some kids eventually. You know, a simple, normal life. No drama and most certainly wouldn't be here."

"Sounds nice. I work a regular nine to fiver and come home to a hot meal. Play catch with the kids in the backyard on a sunny Saturday afternoon. That's what normal people do, right? Wash the car, walk the dog, get the paper." He lowered his voice and caught her eye, "make love until three in the morning, and wake up and keep going on coffee." He faded away as he started to envision this life. The vision quickly faded, and he sighed and looked at Rosie. "I got my diagnosis today."

"What does that look like?" Rosie asked.

"Nothing that can't be managed with meds. Just a bunch of bull shit if you ask me. Just like your diagnosis." Stephan decided it was best he didn't tell Rosie that he had the brain of a killer. He was afraid if she knew, she would fear him. He realized that he didn't want the life she described to him in some virtual reality machine. He wanted it in the real world. Stephan wanted to take Rosie and run away. They could start this life in reality and leave the wretched hospital behind.

"What are you thinking about? You drifted away for a moment." Rosie's voice broke his train of thought.

"I want to kidnap you, break out of this God forsaken place, and never look back. I want to live that life that you talked about. Their machines won't help us. That house . . . with you . . . that would be it. I would be happy and you would be happy. Why couldn't that be our medicine?"

"How would they make money off of that? They won't let us out of here. They will lead you to believe that they will. They will just build more rooms for more patients." She told him with a pitiful tone.

"Fuck! You're right! The little guy always has to lose for the big man to win and line his pockets. In this life . . . we are so damn . . . small." He paused. This realization angered him. "Rosie, I promise someday soon it will be different for us. I'm gonna get us both out of here if it's the last thing I do."

"Don't make promises you can't keep." He turned to her, and gently took both of her hands in his. She gently squeezed back, and gave him a small smile.

"I really will get us out of here. Rosie, we can't truly be together as long as we are in here. I want to be with you, and if you made your perfect world with me, then you obviously want to be with me too. So, I have to at least try. One day, we will both be out of here."

"Stephan, I don't want you to get hurt . . . or worse. No one ever gets out of here."

"Rosie, for you . . . I would give my life if I had to for you to have your freedom." He didn't care about the cameras watching them from the ceiling. Stephan let his lips meet hers for a long, passionate kiss. He wasn't aware that Nurse Adams was watching them on a hologram screen from the nurses station outside of the common room. The nurse knew what she needed to do, and that was to destroy Stephan slowly now that she knew his weakness.

CHAPTER 5

The next morning, Stephan was called to the nurses station before breakfast to start his new medications. He noticed that there were four pills in the little cup that held them. Stephan recalled the doctor telling him that he was starting three medications, and he was prepared to say something about it.

"The doctor said I was starting three medications, not four." He said suspiciously to the nurse.

"The fourth medication is something everyone takes when they're here. It's just a vitamin. You need to take it and quit asking questions." The nurse said as she poured him some water into the same type of biodegradable cup that was used for coffee in the cafeteria. Stephan emptied the small cup of pills into his mouth, and took the water. He drank the tepid water, and gave the empty cups back to the nurse. "Stick out your tongue, and let me see under it please." Stephan tilted his head back slightly, and stuck out his tongue. He made an 'AAAAAHHHHH' sound as he lifted his tongue. The nurse looked in his mouth, inspecting it for any pills left behind. When she was satisfied, she sent him on his way. He turned around and walked back to his room. He closed the door, but didn't latch it completely closed behind him.

He began to dig the pills out from between his cheek, and lower back gums. He crouched down on the floor at the head of his bed and made sure no one was coming down the hall. He proceeded to use his teeth to make a small tear in the bottom corner of his mattress. Stephan stuffed the pills in the hole he made as far as his index finger could shove them. The glowing red eyes watched him silently from the corner. He could feel its pleasure with what he was doing, but the thought of the doctor adding a fourth pill without his knowledge had left an uneasy feeling in the pit of his stomach. He couldn't believe Dr. Krochek added the extra medication, and didn't expect him to have questions about it. As far as Stephan was concerned, he wasn't going to take any pills. He recalled what the doctor said about the process before being put under. His mind then went to Mabel, and it all came together for him. He realized that he couldn't trust what they were giving him to swallow, literally and figuratively. He had to have his mind at its fullest if he was going to keep his promise to Rosie, and he couldn't be sedated and drooling on himself. He needed to find a way out of the terror that was disguised as a hospital.

Later that day, Rosie and Stephan sat on the couch waiting for the group therapy session to start after lunch and quiet time. Marcus wasn't in the corner that day. He was sitting in the chair where Paul usually sat. His hand only rubbed himself slowly over his hospital pants instead of the usual rapid stroking. His mind seemed to be somewhere else. Sliding footsteps were heard from the hallway and Wanda slid into the common room. She stumbled and fell on the couch with Rosie and Stephan. Today she only mumbled, but her tapping had ceased.

"Wanda, what happened to you?" Stephan asked. He was genuinely concerned for her.

"Most of them . . . have left me." She replied quietly, not looking up from the floor.

"What do you mean?" Rosie asked her. Wanda pointed to her head, and looked at Rosie tearfully.

"I'm not feeling . . . like me anymore." Wanda whispered. "They are being . . . stolen from me, and now . . . they are stealing me." Wanda pointed to the doorway of the common room with a shaking hand. Rosie looked at Stephan with slight fear in her eyes.

"Oh my God, Stephan, is this what we are going to become?" She asked him, with worry written all over her face. Stephan looked at Marcus, and then at Wanda. He remembered how they were when he first arrived at the hospital. They had their issues, but at least they were themselves. Everything was changing at a rapid pace. Stephan knew time was running out.

"No, Rosie. It won't be us. I said I would get us out of here, and I'm going to die trying dammit." He said to her quietly. "Did you take your meds?" He asked her.

"Yes . . . didn't you?"

"Promise me . . . you won't say anything."

"You know I wouldn't, Stephan." He leaned over close to her, and gently brushed her hair away from her ear.

"I cheeked mine. I'm not taking them. The first chance I get, I'm dumping them in Nurse Hitler's coffee." He whispered. Rosie quickly looked at him, and her mouth gaped opened. Before she could say anything, he put his hand lightly over her mouth. "I am only supposed to be on three pills, but there were four in my cup, Rosie. I didn't sign up for that shit, and neither did you. Don't take the pills. I'm convinced that the pills we are given here are not what they say they are . . . take a good look at them." He used his head to motion toward Marcus and Wanda. "Remember Mabel?" Rosie nodded her head, and a look of sadness took over her face.

"Stephan, I feel so stuck. They will know if I don't take the pills. They're going to find out that you haven't been yours eventually, and when that day comes . . . you're going to pay for it. I haven't been here that long, but it's common sense. In a day or two when we are supposed to be too messed up to even walk, and we're not . . . they will know." More slow, sliding steps were heard coming toward the room. Paul entered the room, and sat in a random chair. He didn't trace the line up and down his arm anymore. He instantly drifted off to another place in his mind for several minutes, and suddenly came back from his trance. He looked around the room as if he didn't remember how he got there.

"I can't take those pills, and work on getting us out." He whispered.

"Stephan, it's a nice idea, but you're not going to get us out. That's just a pipe dream. It's time to start thinking realistically."

"A life with you . . . that isn't in here . . . is realistic. I just need you to be on the same page."

"If you do happen to find a way, I will go with you, but I'm not going to hold my breath."

"Have a little faith in me . . . in us. I'm going to do this, and I'm going to burn this place to the ground on my way out."

"I wish I could be more like you, Stephan. You're fearless to the point of being reckless. You don't care about the consequences."

"It's not that I don't care about the consequences. I'm just not going down without a fight."

"That's one of your most appealing attributes." Rosie whispered.

"Really? Well, why are you giving me such a hard time then?"

"I don't want to see you get hurt, or have to suffer any horrible consequences because you got caught doing something that could've been avoided."

"If that time comes, that will be on me."

"I'll worry about you." She looked at him with glassy eyes from holding back tears.

"I'll survive everything they have to throw at me. I've made it this far." The conversation had to come to a halt when the sound of Nurse Adams' heels clicking on the tiles approached. She came in the common room with Lily in a wheelchair. She didn't hesitate to start throwing orders.

"Everyone, take a seat. We are going to start the group shortly." She said as she took her seat at the front of the room. Mr. S entered the room almost immediately after she did, and sat down next to her. "Okay, everyone is here. Hello all! We don't have any new faces. I don't think we need introductions today. Mr. S, I will let you take over from here." She said in one breath, not even looking at the group of patients.

"Okay, first I would like to go around the room, and have each person state how they feel today. Let's start with Marcus over there in the corner." Marcus slowly looked up with his mouth hanging open.

"What . . . do you want?" He asked with slightly slurred speech.

"How do you feel today?" Mr. S repeated.

"Ummm . . . not sure. Half the time . . . I can't even get it hard anymore, and I have no motivation to play with myself like I used to . . . I feel like I'm . . .

floating. That's all . . . I'm finished talking now." He told Mr. S quietly. His head drooped slightly, and he stared off into nothing once again.

"All right, thank you for your input. How about you Wanda? How are you feeling today?"

"I'm upset. He took . . . most of them away." She said slowly.

"He?" Mr. S questioned her.

"Krochek. He is . . . taking my friends away. They are going away . . . one by one. They weren't hurting anyone . . . and this makes me angry . . . and sad." "Okay, thank you Wanda. I'm sorry you feel this way, but you know hearing voices isn't the right thing. If it was, we would all hear voices, and we don't. Paul, let's hear from you."

"I don't know how to feel now. Everything is so . . . confusing." His speech was slightly slurred like Marcus'.

"Confusing how?" Mr. S inquired.

"I know I should be feeling a certain way, but I'm just not . . . I'm not me anymore. I know I should be upset about what happened, but I just don't care . . .

I'm numb to all of it."

"Great job Paul. Thank you for sharing. Rosie, how do you feel today?"

"Fine. I feel fine."

"I would like you to be a bit more specific please."

"Well . . . I still hate being here. Is that better?"

"You're here to get help."

"It's help I could've gone the rest of my life without." Rosie's voice shook as she held back the tears. She was already emotional from the conversation with Stephan.

"How have your medications been helping you?"

"I've started to feel . . . lightheaded. I guess it's something I can deal with if the meds are supposed to help."

"Okay . . . thank you for sharing." Mr. S said quietly. "Stephan . . . we can't wait to hear what you have to say." Mr. S looked at him, waiting for some sarcastic remark.

"I'm pretty jacked that I'm here. I'm disturbed at the fact that I was only supposed to start three meds, but there were four in my cute little cup. No one would tell me what that mystery prize was. I was just expected to swallow it, just like I'm expected to swallow this horse shit." At this statement, Nurse Adams cleared her throat loudly and glared at him. "Yeah, yeah . . . I got it." Stephan directed the comment at her.

"The medicine is designed to help you Stephan. You need to take them. They can help you get better." Mr.S moved on quickly. "Lily, How do you feel today?" All she could do to respond was raise her hand slightly off of the arm of the wheelchair. She drooled on herself the same way Mabel did.

"Lily will be proceeding into one of the control rooms today. We all wish her well." Nurse Adams announced to everyone.

"Yes, we wish you well Lily. Thank you, everyone for participating." Mr. S said appreciatively. "I have an exercise I would like everyone to work on in between now and our next group. I would like you to journal something. It could be an original poem, song, or just writing down how you feel. Anything that you are feeling. Unfortunately, you can't have pencils and papers in your rooms, so you will have to write it in here during common room time. Do you have anything to add Nurse Adams?"

"No, I don't." She said. Stephan raised his hand. "What Stephan." Nurse Adams said flatly, waving her hand him.

"Will you and Mr. S be writing something as well?"

"No. This is an exercise for the patients, and we are not patients." Nurse Adams responded snidely.

"So, you think you are better than us because of this?"

"I'm not arguing with you today." She mumbled to Stephan. "This concludes our group. I hope everyone has a great rest of the day." Nurse Adams and Mr. S stood up from their seats, and quickly exited the room with Lily. "What do we do now?" Stephan asked as he clapped his hands together.

"You were riding on the border of getting strapped down again. Adams and Mr. S left in a very big hurry. I wonder what's up with that." Rosie said curiously.

"Maybe they are buying mops for all the drool that's going to be happening soon. No, but seriously . . . I think they have some weird S and M sex with each other, and we both know who the dom is." He said in a low tone. "I'm used to staring at the ceiling of my room, what should we do?" He asked.

"Maybe we should work on that journal exercise." Rosie suggested to him.

"Are you fucking kidding me right now?" Stephan exclaimed, giving her a look of shock.

"No . . . do you have anything better to do? They don't get shit on the television."

"Yeah, let's find a closet that Nurse Satan and Mr. S aren't in, and get naughty." Stephan gave her a wink and Rosie laughed nervously.

"You wish lover boy. I'll go get pencils and paper." Rosie left the room and was gone a mere minute before she was back. She handed Stephan his pencil and paper. The pencils had no erasers because of the small amount of metal that would have to be used to contain it. The hospital didn't want anyone turning it into a weapon for destruction. All they had was long pieces of soft graphite inside a hollow rubber tube. Stephan carefully analyzed the writing utensil, and looked at Rosie.

"Are you serious? They expect us to use this?" He asked her.

"They use the same ones in prisons. Look on the bright side...I'm pretty sure these things make every guy feel awesome about themselves . . . Krochek being the exception, but I'm quite sure he has a micro penis. We have all seen Marcus' glory." Stephan got a good laugh from this.

"God, you are so awesome. Where were you thirteen years ago?"

"Being blissfully unaware that I was crazy, and any of this was going to be my life." She said with slight hostility, and she was quick to change the subject. "So, what are you going to write about."

"My memoirs." Stephan replied with dramatic flair. He always had a creative streak, and he knew exactly what he would write. He would reveal how he felt about the hospital and his wife in the form of poetry. It would have angst and bitterness, because that's how Stephan felt about it all. It would be angry and aggressive. He felt that way, and couldn't act on it. If he had acted on his irritations, nurses, doctors, orderlies and a therapist would have been equalized by now.

CHAPTER 6

That night, the demon whispered loudly to Stephan as it crouched in the chair in the corner. It's glowing, red eyes penetrated the darkness and faintly lit up his room. That's all Stephan could see, even when he closed his eyes. It was nights like this he would have gotten drunk until he passed out. If only he wasn't trapped inside a hospital that wanted to use him as guinea pig for an experiment.

"You hear me now." The being whispered. "Say my name." It beckoned him. Stephan didn't say his name, and he pretended not hear the whispers. He started to think about what he wrote for the group therapy assignment to occupy his mind. A part of him said it was a bad idea to share such an intimate side of himself in front of Nurse Adams. Another part of him wanted to get it all out to help himself feel better, and just say to hell with what she thought. He also thought about the medications that were hidden in the mattress underneath him. The idea of being caught made him nervous. He wondered what would happen if he were to be caught. *'Nurse Satan would have a field day with it all. Would Rosie be questioned? Oh God . . . What would happen to her?'* Stephan's thoughts began to get panicky and frantic. *'I gotta get rid of these pills somehow.'*

He thought to himself. Paranoia washed over him and it kept him awake most of the night. He saw dawn slowly approaching through a small space in between the curtains. For this, he was thankful. This meant he could get the pills out of the mattress and flush them down the toilet. He rolled over on his side with his back to the shadow and stared at the blank, white wall. Stephan eventually drifted off into a light, restless sleep.

It felt as though he was asleep for a mere five minutes when his door was opened and he was being called for breakfast. He reluctantly sat up and put on the yellow slipper socks that the hospital provided and stepped into the hallway. He quickly used the restroom and took his place in line. Rosie quietly slid up behind him.

"Good morning, cowboy. You look like crap." She said cheekily, startling Stephan.

"Yeah, I didn't sleep very well." He said as he rubbed the back of his neck. His hair stuck in all different directions from the tossing and turning.

"I get it. It's this place." She responded with discernment.

"It's more than that."

"You want to talk about it."

"I wish I could, but I'm to the point now that I don't know who is listening that shouldn't be hearing." He told her, letting the paranoia show.

"We should be safe in the cafeteria." She said, humoring his paranoia. They walked silently to the cafeteria and retrieved their breakfast. Stephan made an exception and made a cup of coffee. He knew that he needed to stay awake. In the morning they allowed the patients to have caffeinated coffee. He and Rosie went to their usual table in the corner and sat down. He took a small sip of the coffee.

"Dear God! You were right! Worst coffee ever, and I'm gonna have to choke this cup of liquid shit down just to stay awake!" Stephan exclaimed.

"I had a cup my first day here and I decided I would rather eat vomit."

"Wow . . . that's graphic."

"And liquid shit isn't? So, what kept you awake all night?"

"I think I need to start keeping you in the dark about certain things I'm going to do in the future. I can't implicate you in any way. The less you know, the better. If anything happened to you, I would never forgive myself. I have to get rid of the pills I've cheeked so far. I'll tell you that much."

"I thought you were slipping them to what's her face." Rosie said as she shoved a bite of a pancake in her mouth.

"Yeah, I was, but I think that is just an easy way to get caught. I gotta be smart about this."

"That's true." She responded. Stephan clenched his eyes shut, and took a deep breath. He finished the coffee in just a few gulps, and dropped the empty cup. He made a strange noise in the back of his throat, reached for his juice, and drank the small carton in one gulp.

"God, that was disgusting. They must use the same coffee grounds three days in a row or something."

"Did you learn anything?" Rosie was amused by what she had witnessed.

"Yeah, next time I'll just take a nap." They finished their breakfast, and headed to the common room. Stephan and Rosie went to the place where they hid their written assignments and retrieved them. "Come sit with me, Rosie." Stephan said while patting the seat next to him.

"So are you going to let me read yours before the group, or is it going to be a surprise?" Rosie asked him.

"Well, I actually want to write another thing. The one I wrote already is about the ex-wife. So, it's obviously nothing positive. I kinda want to write something about the Queen of Gingivitis too. You can read them when they're finished. They're not top secret."

"Whoa, two things . . . aren't you a being just a little brown nosing class act?"

"Ouch! I am wounded! I'm more of the class clown, thank you." Stephan put his hand over his heart and let out a loud sigh. He smiled at Rosie. He enjoyed it when she picked at him. It told him that she was on the same level as him.

"Who's the Queen of Gingivitis?"

"Halitosis Hitler, Nurse Satan . . . Adams."

"How many nicknames do you have for her?" Rosie asked.

"Oh . . . I have a feeling they will be never ending. Just like her nasty attitude and breath of torment." Stephen explained.

"What did she do to make you turn against her?"

"Well, when I first got here, she threw open my curtains like she was in a fucking Disney movie. This is no kid's movie and I'm pretty sure the only birds that like her are ones that pick at road kill. Then, when we were on our way back from Montgomery's office . . . I asked her a simple question three damn times, and she ignored me. I was pushed to the point where I had to be in restraints again. She runs this place like a prison and acts all innocent in front of her boss."

"I have seen her do stuff like that to other patients. Believe it or not, Paul was quite unruly when he first got here. He had to learn the hard way. We arrived on the same day. He learned a lot quicker than you obviously. I just figured it was better to stay out of her way. You sir, are very confrontational though, and like to get on her last nerve. Like I said, you don't care about consequences. You go in balls to the wall . . . every time."

"I really do, and she makes it so easy. She has this vein in her forehead that starts to throb. I kinda want to be the one that makes it explode."

"You're really demented. You know that?"

"You realize that we are in a psychiatric hospital." Stephan stated to her notably.

"At least we're in the right place then." They both laughed.

"Let's finish these writing things." Rosie said sighing.

"Sure. It takes longer when you have to write with bendy utensils that are three inches long." Stephan mumbled under his breath, and proceeded to read what he wrote the day before. Again, he felt the bitterness in his words as he reread them. He added some finishing touches to his poem, and glanced at Rosie. She was deep into what she was writing, and clearly wanted it to be a secret at the moment. He turned his attention back to his own paper, and started constructing the second poem he wanted to write. He looked around the room for a minute, and noticed Paul was sitting in the room as well, but was staring into a void only he could see. Stephan laid his head on the back of the couch, and stared at the ceiling in deep thought. He closed his eyes trying to figure out where he should begin. He thought about how the staff treated him when he first arrived. He thought about how Nurse Adams set him up to be put back into restraints. Then the words he wanted to write came to him, and he let the animosity fuel the poem all the way to the end. When he was finished, he looked over at Rosie, and saw that she was staring at him intently.

"Wow. You were in that . . . like . . . really deep. What did you write?" She asked with great curiosity.

"I'll show you mine if you show me yours." He said, wiggling his eyebrows at her.

"Woo . . . sounds like fun."

"Seriously . . . trade?" He asked, offering his poems to her.

"Only if you promise not to laugh." Rosie hesitated.

"I'm an asshole about a lot of things, but I won't be about this." He promised as they exchanged papers. Their smiles faded as they read each others vulnerability and raw emotion. They saw a part of each others heart that neither one of them talked about. When they were finished reading, they gave the papers back to one another. Neither of them said anything right away. Rosie was the first one to finally speak.

"So, the first one is about your ex-wife?"

"Uh, yeah." He answered quietly.

"What exactly happened with her?"

"Well, she said I was coming here to talk to a doctor for some help, but she was really dropping me off. Leaving me here for the long haul. Completely caught me off guard there. When I had my first meeting with Dr. Krochek, she was in his office to let me know she wanted a divorce. Now, I'm probably going to lose my business and house. Blind sided again by the heartless bitch."

"So you're not even officially divorced yet."

"No, I'm waiting for the day when Krochek presents me with the papers, and has me sign them."

"Will you sign them?" She asked with a hushed and nervous tone.

"Pffft! Might as well, I mean, what other choice do I have? That bitch abandoned me in here. That was the only time I have seen her since I've been here. She probably has someone new already, because she wanted a baby. Why would she want a baby with me? I'm apparently fucked up beyond all measures, and women usually don't line up for a guy like that. She thinks she's better than I am, but that's fine. Besides, I have bigger plans going on now that don't include her. She is part of the past as far as I'm concerned. She can write me off, well I can do the same thing, and write her off. I'll start by signing those damn papers. She can have it all, but it will be short lived. When we get out, I'm gonna burn it all down around her."

"Well said, but I think you're being a little hard on yourself. I think you're a catch. You're funny, driven, easy on the eyes. You have your flaws, but so do every other human being on this planet . . . including your wife." Rosie said with a smile. "The second one you wrote, is that the one about the Queen of Gingivitis?"

"Not just her . . . but every staff member here that treats me like I'm just a number. They treat all of us like we are just a number, and we don't matter. As long as they all get paid . . . that's all that matters to them." Stephan responded.

"There is a lot of . . . hate in there."

"Well I don't exactly like these arrogant pieces of work."

"I guess writing about it is better than killing them, or something like that." She added

"Exactly the point." Stephan said. "I won't lie though, I do fantasize about it."

"About what?" Rosie asked.

"Killing certain staff here. In all kinds of different ways." Stephan said quietly, with a small smile. Rosie was quiet for a minute.

"Nurse Adams' reaction to this could be you in restraints again." She finally told him.

"This is gonna be good then. Now, your poem, Rosie. What's up?" Stephan asked.

"Well, I think it's pretty self explanatory."

"It's just so . . . lonely and sad. It's heartbreaking, dear. It makes me wonder what happened to you when you were growing up, and if you ever had anyone that was truly there for you." Stephan looked at her waiting for an answer. Rosie sat there in silence, and refused to give anything away. "You don't have to say anything. Sometimes the past needs to stay right where it's at . . . in the past." "Have you ever wondered that emotional disorders are not something you are born with? Maybe it's the people you are around that drive you to the point of going crazy? If you just had the chance to separate yourself from them, you would be all right." Rosie deeply pondered aloud.

"Yeah, all the time. Except I see a red-eyed demon that talks to me, but I understand what you're saying completely. Knowing how my wife is now . . . perhaps she drove me over the edge with my anger. Maybe she was another reason I drank and got high all of the time. Looking back . . . I can see how we were both unhappy. I should have been the one to leave her a long time ago. I think we married each other out of obligation. We had history, and neither one of us had the guts to start over. It's always a scary thing to travel into the dark and unfamiliar. We went with what was safe and familiar. Hindsight is twenty-twenty though. With all the advancements in technology we still haven't invented a damn time machine." Stephan ranted.

"What would you do with a time machine?"

"Knowing what I know now?" Stephan added.

"Knowing everything, you know now." Rosie added agreeably.

"I would not give Sandy the time of day, and I would find you. I would find Nurse Hitler's mom. Tell her what a rotten shit her daughter is going to be, unless she does something different, like beat her ass more. The most important thing though . . . I would marry you. Give you the life you deserve, and make sure you never have another lonely day again. I don't think we would end up in here if it happened like that."

"Let's invent a time machine." Rosie said.

"Pipe dreams make the world go 'round." They rose from the couch and hid their papers in the spot they chose. As soon as they sat back down, a nurse came in and told them that they needed to go to their rooms. "Well, I guess it's that time. I'll see you at lunch, dear." Stephan said as he inconspicuously gently brushed her hand with his. They walked to their rooms together and stood in their doorways, taking advantage of every minute they didn't have to be shut inside of them. The nurse came around to lock them in and tell them lunch will begin shortly. Stephan did as he usually did and stared out of his window. He saw the green truck leave on its regular run into town. He also observed a new patient being dropped off. He wondered if that's what it was like when he was dropped off. What was it like for the observer when he was kicking and shouting on his way in?

"Another number to be added to the doctors list. Another dollar in his pocket." The demon stood closely behind Stephan. He could feel its breath on the back of his neck. He watched the dark-haired woman beg her husband not to leave her just as he had done with his wife. She didn't fight against the orderlies as he had done. The woman was escorted calmly into the hospital as she sobbed.

"We are all just a number and dollars in his pocket. Once you're here, no one gives a shit about you any more." Stephan finally responded to the shadow. He found himself pitying the woman, because he knew what she was feeling. He had been there, and he was still there. The situation would never get any better for either one of them unless someone did something about it. Stephan was that someone planning to do something about it. He remembered the pills in the mattress. He went over to the head of his bed and sat on the floor. He stuck his finger in the hole that he had made. He could feel the numerous pills, but he heard someone approaching his door. He quickly removed his finger, but in the process two pills fell out. Stephan instantly became jittery. He grabbed both of the pills, and sat on his bed just as his door opened.

"Line up for lunch." A nurse said. She moved along to tell the next patient.

He let out a sigh of relief, and shoved the two pills back into the hole.

"Close! Too close . . ." The demon hissed angrily. It fell backwards, and faded into the dark corner. The pills would have to stay in the mattress for now. He made his way into the hallway to line up for lunch. He stood behind Rosie and ran his fingers through his hair nervously. She glanced at him, and noticed he was perspiring profusely.

"What were you doing in your room that has you all sweaty?"

"I'll tell you in a bit." His heart was still racing from what happened in his room. He wiped away large beads of sweat from his forehead with the sides of his hands. He thought he was caught for sure. When they were sitting at the table, he finally told her what happened.

"Wow, you have to be more careful or you are going to be strapped down for the rest of your time here, and you won't like that."

"I know! I freaked out a little bit . . . my heart is just now going back into normal rhythm!" Stephan exclaimed in hushed voice.

"What were you trying to accomplish?" Rosie asked him as she furrowed her brow.

"I was going to flush them down the toilet." He responded quietly.

"That's a really bad idea. They monitor everything that goes down the toilets, showers and sinks. If pills go down, you would have gotten locked inside the bathroom until a nurse or an orderly opened the door for you. Then you're *really* busted. Those toilets also analyze your urine. Everything from a drug test for the employees . . . to a urinary tract infection for the patients. So if pills go down, you're definitely screwed."

"Damn, good to know. I'm glad you told me that before I did that. So, mattress stash it is until I can figure out something else."

"I didn't hear that." Rosie said, looking away.

"Oh right. So let's change the subject. Why don't they let us outside? Even if it's a fenced in area . . . it would still be outside, and as Mr. S puts it . . . therapeutic."

"Not sure. It's a good idea though. Maybe you should bring it up today."

"Nah. I know why they don't let us outside. It's because they don't really care. How much do you want to bet, that the state gives them money for having patients here? The more patients they have, the more money this place makes. Probably another reason why no one leaves once they're here." Stephan said, being realistic and political.

"I wouldn't bet on that, because I'm almost guaranteeing you're right."

"How come you know so much about this place? How do you know they monitor what goes in the toilets, and all the other stuff that you know?"

"Well, my mother started coming here when I was a teen. That was back in the day when patients used to be released on medication. Before this perfect world, virtual reality BS. She told me some things about this place. The technology was starting to advance the last time they allowed her to be released. She told me how they were starting this experiment."

"Where is your mother now?" Stephan asked her.

"She's actually . . . here." Rosie's voice broke a bit.

"What? When . . . Why?"

"When she heard about the perfect world stuff needing testers, she didn't hesitate to volunteer. I was twenty two when she came here for that. When they tried to wake her when the testing was over, she never came out of the trance. They decided to leave her in the machine, and she's been that way for thirteen years now. This is her home now."

"What about your dad?" Stephan asked.

"He was gone the minute my mom told him she was pregnant. Just a dead beat loser. I was probably better off without him."

"Oh . . . one of those guys. Sorry. So, your Aunt dropped you off. I'm assuming she raised you because of your mom being in and out of here." Rosie nodded her head and Stephan grew quiet. "How was that for you?"

"She had her own daughters to worry about, I came last. I eventually ended up in the system . . . you know . . . foster care. I learned to survive though. Foster care was better than living with my aunt."

"You shouldn't have had to . . . just survive. You never should have been in places like that. You deserved people who would stick by you." Stephan said angrily.

"She couldn't wait to bring me here, and prove I'm just like my mother. She definitely had an opinion about my life then. I got to tell her how I felt about her and my cousins before she left though. That felt really good."

"It sounds like she's the one that needs to be here." Rosie smiled at Stephan, and took his hand. "Seems this place just likes to screw people over in all kinds of ways."

CHAPTER 7

Stephan did his usual routine during quiet time, and stared through his window. There was no patient having a cigarette today, but he did see the truck come from behind the building again. It bounced down the gravel driveway, and towards town. He wondered if he could get his hands on the truck and escape. The shadow billowed up from the floor like smoke in the corner. Its red eyes gleamed. Stephan caught a glimpse of it out of the corner of his eye, and he smiled and sighed.

"Say my name." It ordered Stephan with an eerie whisper.

"What do you want from me?" He asked it quietly, without turning around.

"You know what I want. Don't fight it." It whispered again. Stephan allowed a bigger smile to spread across his face.

"I don't think you're in the position to tell me what to do."

"We shall see about that." It warned ominously, and faded into the corner. The shadow had never touched Stephan before. He didn't think it would start now. According to the doctor, the demon was something in his head. How can something in his head do any harm to a physical being? When quiet time was over, he was back in the common room. He and Rosie sat on the couch together as they had done since the first day they met. Since she had met Stephan, she didn't feel the need to hug her knees in comfort anymore. Paul sat in his usual corner and he stared into a blank space, waiting for his turn to become a drooling mess. Marcus had one hand under his gown, cupping his genitals. He sat in the same place that he always had in previous groups. Stephan saw what they were becoming, and he looked at Rosie.

"Are you still taking the pills?" He asked her.

"Yeah . . . I'm sorry but I'm not as brave as you."

"Oh, Rosie. Please . . . I can't see you turn into . . ." He couldn't find the right word to describe what the pills turn the patients into. Knowing that she was taking the pills, and he would have to see her the way Mabel was, bothered him immensely. He knew he had to act fast if there was any hope of taking her with him. He didn't know how he was going to get to Rosie, and escape from the hospital. He heard heels clicking against the tiles. Nurse Adams directed a wheelchair with Wanda in it. He looked away quickly and stared at the floor. The nurse placed the wheelchair with the rest of the group and left the room.

"Dear Lord, Wanda. Can you speak?" Rosie asked.

"Yeee . . . aaahh." Wanda managed to slur. Drool dribbled from her mouth with her response. Stephan didn't find it funny anymore, knowing that this would be Rosie if she kept taking the medication.

"Are you okay?"

"Goooo . . . gooonnne." Her voice trailed off. Her eyes became distant and sad for a moment, but quickly went blank. She had forgotten the person she used to be. Rosie and Stephan knew she was talking about the voices being all gone.

"Rosie, if you keep taking those pills, that will be you. Shitting yourself and drooling. I can't stand it."

"I don't want it either, but what choice do I have?" Rosie argued.

"We do have a choice." Stephan finally said. "I will make this happen. I won't let you become like some pants shitting zombie." After this comment they got their papers and sat in silence, and waited for the group to start. After five minutes, Nurse Adams' heels were heard on the floor once again. She entered the common room with Mr. S behind her with the woman that Stephan observed from his window earlier.

"Good afternoon everyone. We have a new patient. Everyone . . . this is Fiona." Nurse Adams said. She went around the room and introduced everyone to the new patient. Stephan stayed in his seat and listened in silence. "I believe Mr. S gave you some homework yesterday. Some are exempt from the assignment due to their mental state. Fiona, you weren't here for it, so you can listen." Nurse Adams sat down and Stephan raised his hand.

"Yes . . . Stephan." Nurse Adams sighed.

"You said this was homework . . . well this isn't home to me . . . so does that mean I'm one of those that are exempt?"

"Nice try." She responded with a smirk. "Mr. S, if you would like to take it from here."

"You all were asked to write a poem, song or just a journal entry to share. Before you are asked to read, I would like Wanda to vocalize her feelings as best she can. Wanda How do you feel today?" Wanda's blank expression was replaced with brief awareness to her reality.

"Sssaad." She said slowly.

"Why do you feel sad?" Mr. S questioned Wanda.

"Gooonnne." Wanda tried to raise her hand to point to her head, but only managed to get her hand four inches off of the arm of the wheelchair, and flopped it back down.

"Well, it's for the best Wanda. You are not supposed to be hearing voices like that. It's our job to remedy that. Thank you for sharing. Paul, I would like to hear what you have written now. Please, come closer to the group." Mr. S motioned with his hand for Paul to come out of the corner. Paul continued to sit there, and stare blankly at the floor. His knuckles were white from clasping the arms of the chair. "Paul!" Mr. S called again.

"Oh for crying out loud." Nurse Adams mumbled. She walked over to Paul, and grasped his shoulder, "Paul! Mr. S is speaking to you!" His gaze slowly shifted to the therapist, but he said nothing.

"Paul, did you write something?" The therapist asked. He continued to stare, until a small moan came from the back of his throat. His hands suddenly released their hold from the arms of the chair, and Paul helplessly slid to the floor like a rag doll. Nurse Adams put her hands on her hips and sighed. She was quick to leave the room, and come back with a wheelchair.

"Stevens, give me a hand, will ya?" She asked as she bent over Paul's limp muscular body. Mr. S did his best to assist the nurse. She eventually had to call an orderly for assistance. Mr. S was useless in the lifting department. The other patients sat and watched the ordeal. Rosie and Stephan were horrified at the sight. Eventually Paul was safely put into a wheelchair, and the group session could commence. "How do you even call yourself a man?" Nurse Adams mumbled to Mr. S. He just bowed his head and turned red as he returned to his seat to continue the session.

"Where were we . . . Marcus, what did you write?"

"Didn't . . . do it." He slurred. "Is this . . . hiiiigh schoooool? Yooooouuu suck . . . soooo, suck . . . my . . . liiiimp . . . diiiick." Mr. S was thrown off guard by this. He didn't expect Marcus to have maintained his off-putting personality with as medicated as he was. He didn't want to agitate him any further though. He seemed to be one step behind Paul.

"Uh . . . Th . . . thank you for sharing Marcus." He stumbled over his words. He already felt emasculated by Nurse Adams and Marcus' remarks added more to his humiliation.

"Yooouuu're weeelcooome." Marcus responded with a wayward grin. His chin fell to his chest and he blankly stared at the floor again.

"Let's hear from Rosie." Stephan looked at Rosie, and noticed she was a little nervous.

"Okay . . . so I have to read it in front of everyone . . . I just thought, I would hand it to you, and that would be the end of it."

"It is therapeutic to face our fears and to be bold, Rosie." Mr. S explained gently.

"All right, you seem to know what you're talking about . . . so . . . here it goes. I wrote a poem." She paused. Her hands began to shake nervously. "I mourn my insignificance in idle silence. Weeping the pained tears of questioning. My heart awaiting for false hopes to become reality. Awaiting a return to what once was. Lost in a dark illusion, roaming aimlessly. Forgotten and faded in a black curtain of despair. I am oblivious to the light that quietly beckons. My heart of stone chooses to stay to dwell in the confusion and torment. These tears are torture, gnawing and gnashing at my soul. I am left with a small glimmer of hope, the hope to arise from the ashes again. A rebirth is distant. I know this. Wailing out of frustration. I scream to the Heavens, asking God, why? Why has this turmoil plagued my already shattered and blackened heart? Why must my mind be riddled with chaos? I become camouflaged in the overwhelming sadness that is my being. I mourn my insignificance alone, but with purpose. I am left forsaken, to ponder the questions. That's . . . the end." She finished, and set the paper, face down on her lap.

"Rosie, you express some deep feelings of sadness and loneliness. Are they feelings from your past?" Mr. S asked.

"Something like that."

"Can you elaborate on that at all?" He pushed her for an answer.

"Look, I did the assignment. I don't wanna talk about where the words came from. So how about you just thank me for sharing already, and move along."

"Okay. Clearly you're not comfortable with talking about certain things in an open group. Thank you for sharing. Fiona, I know you didn't write anything, but if you would like to tell us about yourself or anything like that, this is your time." Mr. S told the new patient.

"Ummm . . . well? I'm nine years old, and I'm going into fourth grade. My brother says I'm going to hate my teacher, because he had her, and he says she's mean. I like chocolate ice cream with rainbow sprinkles, and I think my mommy should give me a sister to play with." Fiona rambled like a child.

"I like chocolate ice cream with sprinkles too." Mr. S said to Fiona with a genuinely kind smile. Stephan stared at the woman with his mouth half open. He couldn't believe what he just heard. The woman had to be fifty years old. Mr. S snapped him out of his astonishment by announcing his turn, "and last, but not least, Stephan."

"I actually wrote two things."

"You only had to write one." Mr. S said flatly. He sounded annoyed by Stephan.

"I had good muses, and it fueled the creativity for which I cannot be held responsible for. I felt compelled to write two things. To save you asking questions afterwards, the one I'm reading now is about my ex-wife. The second one I wrote . . . is dedicated to all of you . . . hardworking staff." Stephan cleared his throat obnoxiously. "I see Hell through tunnel vision. The devil's hand around my throat. I try to twist away and fight in the darkness. Battles others see in their darkest nightmares are my everyday reality. I attempt to rise above the demons triumphantly only to open doors into more fire. My skin is scarred and I can barely breathe. I grasp to consciousness by a thread. I refuse to let the hell hounds take me. My soul is hanging in a noose as a possession of the devil that created this monster. Just another day that I can't save myself. I can only delay the inevitable. Today's salvation is tomorrow's damnation. I'm holding my own broken heart. Wandering . . . bleeding and numb. Trapped in the limbo of my own mind. Demons are lying dormant, waiting for a moment of weakness. Waiting to feast on the remains of my humanity. This wasteland is pulverizing, arid and lifeless. Forsaken to go alone as the demons tear me down further. I can't escape what you created for me. Someday I'll find a way to leave you here in my place." There was a moment of silence when Stephan finished reading.

"You said this was about your ex-wife. Do you blame her for your condition and for you being here?" Mr. S finally asked.

"Well, yes. I do blame her for me being here. She is the one that signed me in here against my will, and left me here to die without any regard as to how I would feel about it. However, my diagnosis isn't her fault, but the shitty way she handled it . . . now that is her fault."

"Have you thought that maybe she did it to, look out for you? That she did it, because she cared about you?"

"If that brainless nitwit cared about me, she would have visited me other than the time she came here to tell me she wanted a divorce."

"It seems like you have some issues with that, and name calling isn't going to change her mind on whether or not she loves you. You can't make someone love you." Mr. S said quietly, glaring at Stephan over the rims of his glasses.

"It's like you're fucking my ex-wife, Mr. S. The way you stick up for her . . . it's as if you love her or something." Stephan joked, rolling his eyes.

"No, I don't know Sandy. As far as my personal life is concerned, that's not up for discussion."

"Now, I never said her name. How do you know her name is Sandy?" Stephan sat forward on the couch, and rested his forearms on his knees. He stared at Mr. S, not breaking eye contact. Things between the two men suddenly became intense and serious.

"I . . . I know her name from your chart. Now you said you wrote a second poem. Let's hear that now." Mr. S was quick to change the subject. Stephan studied Mr. S menacingly in silence for a few seconds. He observed the nervous behavior of the therapist. He saw the sweat begin to form on his brow and upper lip. His hands became shaky, and his voice was trill when he spoke.

"Okay, let me read that now." Stephan stared down Mr. S again for a moment, and turned his attention to the paper in his hands. He snapped the stiff paper, and obnoxiously cleared his throat again. "Feed upon the sulfur of a sinner's soul, while I wait in the shadows to bring you into the abyss of honesty to face your dishonor. Latching yourself to merciless torment, disguised as decency. I will take what's left of your soul and consume it as my own. Sulfur of a sinner's soul, flawed and arrogant. Evil like the demons who have granted you their false pardon. You have joined the darkness, and I'm waiting for you."

"That sounds a little . . . threatening." Mr. S said, realizing he could finally have the upper hand over Stephan.

"It's just a poem . . . you know . . . how I feel. You know feelings, right Mr. S?" Stephan let a sadistic grin slowly creep upon his face.

"It still sounds a little malicious."

"And it's still just a little poem. Are you threatened by words? I can't help how I feel, just like you. Just like my ex-wife."

"Okay, well I believe that this should be taken up with Dr. Krochek." Mr. S said, trying to regain his authority.

"Oh, please do. Maybe I can discuss how you are schticking my wife with him as well." Stephan sat back and waited for his response.

"Thank you for sharing Stephan. Nurse . . . Adams. I think you should . . .

take it from here." Mr. S began to gather his papers and folders.

"Thank you for participating everyone. Everyone who has a paper, please pass them to me. We would like to keep what you have written on file with the doctor. Unless Mr. S has another assignment for you . . ." She looked at him and he shook his head, "this concludes group today." They both stood up and Nurse Adams escorted Wanda out of the room and Mr. S wheeled Paul to his room.

"Oh my God! Stephan, I thought you were gonna be in your restraints again!" Rosie exclaimed.

"No, I pulled back. I can't afford to lose time like that." Stephan said quietly.

"What was up with you and Mr. S?"

"I'm not an idiot. He said her first name, and I know someone like him wouldn't be looking at my chart. He doesn't have the authority. He's Sandy's new someone . . . that pussy is the new boyfriend. What a fucking downgrade! Yeah, I'm crazy . . . but I'm not stupid, and at least I'm not some noodle armed geek. Fuck it. She downgraded, and I upgraded. So, that's all that matters to me. I just hate his face even more now though." He looked at Rosie and smiled. The compliment he said about him upgrading caused her olive cheeks to blush.

"Just let them be. There isn't much you can do about it from here anyway, right." Rosie looked at Stephan. She felt fear and excitement when she saw the evil look spread across on his face. It was as if he had more of a motive to get out of Euphoria Hills now. Stephan was pushed into a dark place, and she knew he would stop at nothing to get out now.

CHAPTER 8

Stephan's day began with a slight strain between him and Rosie at breakfast. She noticed his eyes were almost black from his inner rage. He didn't say much, and she was afraid to ask what was on his mind. Stephan had finally reached his breaking point. He had thought he reached that point when he was put in the hospital, but he was only teetering on the edge. Knowing his wife was with someone else before the divorce papers were signed made him think of many different scenarios. He thought that his placement in the hospital was part of an elaborate plan to get him out of the picture. This way, his wife and Mr. S could be together without him getting in the way. He also thought that they could've been having an affair before he was in the hospital. All these thoughts drove him more insane, but he gritted his teeth and smiled at what he would do if given the chance. He tried to overpower the 'what ifs' with plans of the demise of everyone he felt has done him wrong. It gave him a demented sort of peace of mind. He had been pushed over the edge, and he was falling. It was only a matter of time before he would hit the bottom and completely break. The demon sang quietly in the corner.

A serenade of Stephan's defeat. The closer Stephan slipped closer to the darkness in his mind, the more he felt himself giving in to the being.

He sat next to Rosie on the couch in common room after breakfast. He had his hands folded together neatly, and rested them on his lap. Rosie tried to think of something to say that would possibly bring him back.

"So, are you still cheeking your pills?" She whispered.

"Yes. I'm so determined to get us out of here. More than ever now." He told her in a strange, monotone voice. This was a different side of Stephan, and she was sure that she didn't like it.

"What's the plan for if we get out?"

"Not if . . . when. I have a few . . . errands to run, but then we go off the grid."

"We could go to the mountains or the beach." She told him excitedly.

"Why not both? We should probably keep on the move as much as possible until we find a place that's secure."

"I agree, maybe another country then." She lightly touched his arm. He looked at her and smiled. It was the smile that he had before the darkness took over.

"I'm so glad you're being supportive." He told her sincerely. They heard heels clicking closer to the doorway of the common room. Nurse Adams poked her head in.

"Stephan, it's time for you to see Dr. Krochek. Come with me." She ordered harshly. Stephan slid off of the couch, and slowly followed the nurse with a confidant swagger.

"Can I expect any indecency from you today?" She asked.

"Not today, but ask again tomorrow. You never know with me. Now how about we just walk in silence . . . I've been . . . thinking a lot today." He replied quietly.

"Ha . . . *you* want silence? Amazing." Nurse Adams jerked his arm, and squeezed as she usually did. She led him down the corridor. When they were inside Dr. Krochek's office, there was a man in a suit sitting in front of the desk. Nurse Adams was asked to wait outside. When she saw the man in the suit, she didn't hesitate to obey her superior. Stephan stood in the middle of the room, and wondered what was going to happen.

"So who is this guy in the penguin attire, an attorney?" Stephan said smiling.

"As a matter of fact, yes. He is a divorce lawyer, and he is representing your wife." Dr. Krochek explained bluntly. Stephan's smile quickly faded.

"Well then, I guess that means I probably have some papers to sign. Let's get it over with." He stomped over to his usual chair and flopped down hard.

"I am obligated to explain to you that upon signing these papers, you are surrendering all of your assets to your wife. Because of your . . . situation, you are entitled to nothing. She will get the house and everything in it. Luckily, the two of you had no children, so there won't be any dispute in that area. I understand that you had a successful furniture business. That will also become hers since you are no longer of sound mind and won't be able to run it. Do you understand what I'm telling you right now, Mr. Cranston?" The lawyer asked.

"So, all my hard work . . . the money I invested to get that business started . . . is just gone. I bought that house! That woman never worked a day in her life!

She just gets it all though."

"I know it's not ideal, but that's correct." The lawyer responded pitifully. Stephan felt the blind rage building again when he thought about Mr. S' hands all over what he had started. He worked hard to keep everything going for Sandy and their future together. He could deal with losing his wife since he met Rosie, but now he was losing his home and business. The only thing he would have left after signing the papers would be Rosie. He had to think if he really approved with losing it all. He also came to the realization that he didn't have a choice. His situation wasn't ideal, and didn't give him any standing in this argument. All the odds were against him, and he had no chance of winning.

"Give me the damn papers. Bitch can have it all, and I hope it all burns to the ground with them both in it." Stephan mumbled.

"Both of them?" Dr. Krochek questioned him curiously.

"Oh yeah, haven't ya heard? Mr. S is doin' my ex-wife now. Which means his fat sausage fingers will be all over my business . . . my home. He can go ahead and have my sloppy seconds as far as Sandy is concerned, but my business . . . he did nothing to earn it. It's all gonna be handed him just because of the hole he is sticking his dick into."

"Won't be yours anymore, so you won't have any say in whose fingers are all over it." The lawyer interjected impudently.

"You need to shut the fuck up because you're really not helping! You look like a stupid penguin in that suit, and I wanna slap your bald head after it's sunburnt." Stephan said, pointing his finger at the attorney. The attorney scowled and nervously straightened his tie.

"Mr. S is not having relations with your ex-wife. That would be inappropriate due to the fact you're a patient here. Even once she is your ex . . . it would still be inappropriate and frowned upon." Dr. Krochek explained.

"I'm sure some written rule is going to stop them from keeping each other warm at night. If it worked that way, there would be no crime. Oh hey! Don't kill that guy . . . someone wrote it down that you can't!" Stephan challenged Dr. Krochek.

"I think this is another paranoid delusion. You need to think realistically." Dr. Krochek said calmly, trying to bring Stephan back down to reality.

"I am being *very* realistic, and that's kinda why I'm so pissed off. But anyway, papers . . . signing. Lets move this shit party along, and get the short, bald penguin outta here." Stephan looked at the attorney, "he needs to get back on his iceberg, because I really hate his face and I kinda wanna rearrange it. Although, that would be a favor to him, considering what I'm seeing at the moment." The attorney pulled out an electronic tablet that had a stylus attached to it.

"Okay, I explained to you what happens when you sign. Sign by the X. Your signature will be copied everywhere else it needs to go. Once it's signed, it's official, and you will never have to see my . . . bald . . . penguin face again, or your ex-wife. Considering she has already signed." The attorney handed him the device. Stephan reluctantly signed by the X, and shoved it back at him violently.

"Okay, why are you still here? Don't you have an egg to incubate with your ass?" Stephan used his hands to motion for the lawyer to leave. At that gesture, he quickly stood up and gathered his coat, hat and briefcase. He nodded his head at Dr. Krochek, and put the hat on his head. He left the office hurriedly to get away from the hostile situation. It was just Stephan and Dr. Krochek sitting in the room.

"I would like to talk about the poems you wrote in the last group therapy session, one in particular." He paused and pulled out the electronic tablet from a filing cabinet drawer. "We finally managed to get all of your information transferred to a permanent database. It says here that you wrote a poem about the staff here, and you don't like the way they . . . we make you feel. I have read both of the poems, and as much as you are talented . . . you are a rather disturbed individual. Writing these types of things is what's going to keep you here."

"It was a trap. It was a damn set up! I see it now. Tell us that groups are a safe place where we can express ourselves, and when we do, you use it against us! Tell me doc, how much do you get paid per patient? How much money does the government give you? Do more patients in your experiment mean more money?

That's why you gotta make us all look as crazy as possible, you son of a bitch!

Give us all some bull shit diagnosis . . . just enough to keep us here! I mean good God! I'm not saying I'm sane, but I don't think it's anything so bad to keep me here as long as you say. That goes for everyone out there too! I think a monkey could do your job better!" Stephan stared down Dr. Krochek, and imagined himself standing up, grabbing the desk lamp, and hitting Dr. Krochek across the jaw with it. He saw the good doctor spitting out blood and teeth. He was weeping uncontrollably, and unable to speak. At the vivid image, Stephan started to laugh.

"No one was trapping you." The doctor interrupted his train of thought, and his laughter stopped abruptly.

"You seem to be condemning me for my honesty. You don't know what it's like to be on this side of things . . . to just be a patient . . . a number. As much as you don't want to acknowledge the patients as human beings, a part of you has to when we are the ones keeping bread on your table. So, you like the fact that I wrote what I did. Now you have another nail to stick in my coffin, and dollar in your pocket. You already have my serial killer brain pattern." Stephen crossed his arms, and sat back in the chair while he broke eye contact with the doctor.

"You were sent here because you needed psychiatric help. We have the means for treating your conditions. This way, you won't be a burden to society."

"Burden to society? BULL SHIT! You're going to take away reality when you should be teaching ways to deal with everything that's happening in reality. Why can't you just monitor me on some meds for awhile, and let me back into the real world?"

"We have tried that approach in the past. People go off of their medications, and end up in here all over again." Dr. Krochek explained. "Now, how have you been feeling with the new medication?"

"Fine." Stephan responded.

"Just . . . fine? Do you feel any difference in your moods? How do your anxiety and irritability seem to be doing?"

"Everything is fine. They seem to be working."

"Do you feel any lightheadedness . . . dizziness?"

"No. Am I supposed to be?" Stephan looked at the doctor suspiciously.

"What is the fourth pill that every patient gets here?"

"A vitamin."

"I really want to believe you, but I don't think I can." Stephan slumped in the chair and stared at the ceiling.

"You have to take the medication. Have you been taking the pills?" Dr. Krochek asked.

"Of course I have. What other choice is there?" The doctor studied Stephan for a moment.

"Well, I would like to see you again in a couple days. By then, we should definitely know if and how the medications are taking effect." The doctor asked for Nurse Adams to come back into the office, and escort Stephan back to the patient unit. Once they were there, Nurse Adams turned to him.

"Don't you think that just because you had a bad time with Dr. Krochek, it gives you the right to pull any of your usual shenanigans." She took a seat behind the desk at the Nurses Station. He rolled his eyes at her as he made his way to the Common Room. Rosie was waiting for him on the couch. He sat next to her, but didn't say anything right away.

'I think I held it together well in front of Dr. Krochek.' Stephan thought to himself.

"What did the good doctor have for you today?" Rosie asked, breaking the silence between them.

"Lies on top of more lies." He mumbled. He glanced at Rosie, "I signed my life away today. The divorce is final."

"I see. How do you . . . feel about that?" Rosie looked down, and nervously folded her hands together.

"I lost everything. My house . . . my business. All of it . . . gone with a signature." His voice faded.

"I'm sorry." She whispered. She couldn't think of anything else to say. She figured she would let him talk when he was ready.

"I don't care about losing Sandy, not anymore. I'm working through that surprisingly well. I'm thinking maybe I didn't love her as much as I thought that I did. The thing I find most disturbing is I think it was all a set up. She sent me here so she could have it all, and there wouldn't be a fight. She's a selfish bitch. I wouldn't put it passed her at this point considering how she tricked me, and waited until I was here to divorce me. Let's not forget my strong suspicions about her new boyfriend."

"Do you really think she's that underhanded to do something like that to you?"

"I definitely think she's fuckin' Mr.S." He thought out loud.

"You're going to tear yourself up dwelling on all this shit, Stephan. Maybe you should just let it all go. Concentrate on what's going on here and now, and what you need to do. Don't you want to get us out of here?" Rosie was saying anything to distract him.

"Dr. Krochek said what I wrote for the group assignment was threatening so . . . I don't think I'll be getting out anytime soon with his blessing."

"I honestly don't think anyone ever gets out of here with a doctor's blessing, Stephan." She looked at him and smiled. "Welcome to the Hotel California. You can check out anytime you like, but you can never leave." She sang to him, trying to lighten his mood. Stephan ignored her folly. He wasn't in the mood to goof around like he usually would have been.

"We're gonna get out though. We don't need the permission of a doctor for our freedom." The idea of getting out of the hospital had Stephan thinking of how he could make it happen. He had to find a way to get his and Rosie's information. It needed to look as if they were never at the hospital. In order to do that, he would have to find a way into Dr. Krochek's office where the tablets were kept.

CHAPTER 9

"I have a surprise for you." Rosie discreetly handed Stephan a small, flat rectangular metal plate.

"Thanks! It's what I've always wanted!" Stephan exclaimed sarcastically.

Rosie rolled her eyes and laughed while she shoved him lightly with her shoulder.

"Listen, Doofus!" She leaned over, and quieted her voice. "When you go to your room tonight, look down at your door handle. I'm sure you're smart enough to figure out what I'm getting at when you see it." Rosie straightened back up again. Stephan held the piece of metal in a semi open palm with a perplexed look on his face. He was slightly intrigued as to what Rosie was talking about. What could this simple piece of metal mean? The curiosity about the mundane item kept his mind off of everything else throughout dinner and the rest of the night. Rosie didn't bring up the item again, or what it was for either. Stephan enjoyed the mystery. Things were better when Nurse Adams left for the evening, and the night staff began their shift. There weren't many who worked, and the ones that were there didn't take the job too seriously. Everyone that still had their wits about them could tell the young, handsome orderly and the perky, blond nurse was sleeping with each other. They would be entertained with each others company and petty arguments. The other orderly would make himself at home on the couch in the common room in front of the television. He usually dozed off during infomercials or something else he was able to find on the hospital's satellite television. The other nurse would fall asleep at the desk with her feet propped up while doing crossword puzzles. No one bothered doing the mandated hourly checks on the patients. They figured they all slept the whole night through, and there was no point. Another eventful night at the institute. Ten o'clock rolled around and it was time for the patients to go to their rooms. Stephan and Rosie slowly walked to their rooms together. Upon their departure, she gave him a knowing look as she headed to her room. Stephan pulled the piece of metal from his pants pocket, and analyzed his door handle. He looked at Rosie, and watched as she pulled out a duplicate piece of metal. She inserted it into the grooves around the latch of her door. She gave him a small smile and a wave. Then she disappeared inside of her dark room. He looked down at his piece of metal again, and carefully slid it into the grooves of the strike plate around the latch. He saw that it prevented the door from automatically locking when it shut behind him. That's when he knew of Rosie's intentions. He heard a nurse approaching, he quickly dodged into his room, and quietly closed his door. He stood with his back against the wall for a moment and looked around the room. The demon stood in the corner by a vent in the wall, and pointed to it with a long, bony finger. It had a wide, eerie smile on its face. It was displaying its happiness for Stephan's defiance. Thanks to the demon, he finally knew how he was going to get rid of the pills. He had never seen it smile like that before, but he took it as an indication that it was trying to help in its own twisted way for its own motives. He made his way over to his bed, and crawled under the blankets just as a flashlight came in through the small window of his door. The staff was making their only round to see if the patients were in their beds. It would be the only time they would check for the night. Stephan quietly waited in his bed for a few minutes to be sure the staff finished their nightly routine. When everything was quiet out in the hall, he slid out of bed. He went to the corner of his mattress where he stashed his pills. He had to tear the mattress a bit more to get all of the medications out, but he managed to get them all. He held the handful of pills in the palm of his hand, and stared at them for a second. He was sure a good way to get rid of them would be to shove them into the vent in the wall. He started to walk toward the vent when his door suddenly cracked open. Stephan froze, and felt the blood drain from his face. He thought for sure that he was caught, until he saw that it was Rosie. She slipped into the room, and closed the door silently behind her.

"What are you doing?" She asked in a low whispered.

"I'm taking care of a loose end." He croaked when he found his voice again. He turned around and crouched down in front of the vent. Stephan was still shaking from thinking he was caught. With trembling hands, he slid a pill through a slot at the bottom of the vent. He waited to hear the tink of it landing, and began sticking more through. By now, Rosie was crouched down next to him, watching him follow through with his plan.

"Good idea, but I still think they are going to notice when you don't start drooling on yourself." Rosie said quietly.

"We'll be out of here before that happens." He told her confidently, as he dropped more pills into the slot.

"Well, I've been feeling strange after night meds tonight." She looked away from the vent, and at Stephan. "I think the pills are beginning to kick in for me."

"Then I guess I don't have that much time since you insist on taking the damn things." He replied, momentarily stopping what he was doing to look at her. Rosie gave him a pitying half smile, and he looked away to shove the last few pills through the slot. He looked at Rosie again, and lightly stroked her cheek. He swept a stray lock out of her face, and leaned in for a quick kiss. He stood up and helped her off of the floor. They made their way to the single bed, and lie side by side facing each other. Stephan kissed her again, but this time deeper and with more passion. He allowed his hands to wander, and slid his hands down her back. He stopped at her bottom, and squeezed lightly. Rosie returned the affection by wrapping her arms around him. She let out a small moan in the back of her throat and pressed herself into him. Stephan proceeded to slide his hands to the back of her thigh, and pulled her leg between his and drew her closer into him. They both forgot where they were while they lie in each others embrace, and kissed one another deeply. The adrenaline welled up inside each of their chests. The world was spinning for both of them, and before he knew what he was doing, Stephan started to pull up her hospital gown, but stopped.

"Are you okay with this?" He asked shakily.

"Yeah. Why wouldn't I be?" She said, opening her eyes.

"Just wanted to make sure." He continued to kiss her with a passion he had never felt before, and lift her gown. She in return began to lift his, and soon they were both seeing each other in their fleshy vulnerability. He kissed down her neck, and cupped her breast, bringing every nerve ending to life for a new sensation. A quake of a chill ran throughout her whole body, and every sense was awakened in a way that she thought only possible by a god. Stephan ran his hand between her legs, and she bit his lip gently, and dug her nails slightly into his back to stay quiet. She began to writhe and shudder, and began to breathe heavily. Rosie couldn't take it any longer. She rolled him on his back and pressed her lips to his as she straddled him. She held his arms above his head and wove her fingers into his, and put him inside her. They simultaneously let out groans of ecstasy. She bit his lower lip a bit harder this time, and slowly moved her hips up and down as she rocked back and forth. Stephan gently grabbed her around the waist and upper back and flipped her over. Now, he was looking down on her and kissed the curves of her collar bone. She breathed more heavily and tangled her fingers through his hair, and ran her fingers along his facial stubble. She met him with his every thrust as she wrapped her legs around him. He was deep inside her as he came. "Fuck . . . Already?" He whispered. Rosie stifled a laugh. "It's okay, we can go again. We have all night."

They made love like it was the end of the world, and they were the last humans that were ever going to make love on the earth. When they finally became exasperated, they held each other for the rest of the time they had together.

"That was better than what I ever had with anyone else. With you, everything is better." Stephan finally whispered.

"I know exactly what you mean." She replied back to him. He kissed her on the forehead.

"Rosie, tell me about you." He said.

"What do you want to know? My middle name and stuff?" She answered him coyly. She knew what he meant, she didn't want to have the conversation that he did, definitely not right now.

"I want to know the Rosie behind what you wrote. The Rosie that you hide from everyone." They were both silent for a long minute.

"Why do you want to talk about stuff like that? It's not a very good story." She responded.

"Because I want to know the good and what obviously is the bad . . . you told me about your mom, aunt and how your dad split. What was foster care like?"

"I had to share a room with a complete stranger, and I wasn't sure if she was going to runaway after stealing all of my shit, or murder me in my sleep. That's sugar coating it for you. Let's just leave it at that, okay? Let's not ruin tonight."

"All right, you had to have had some good places."

"Nothing good ever happens in those places, Stephan." He decided that the subject was starting to get too sensitive for Rosie, and that he should back off.

"Just know, if you ever need someone . . . I'm here." Stephan told her. He held her tighter, and she rested her head onto his chest. He lightly stroked her shoulder length hair.

"I know, and the same goes for you." She snuggled even closer into his chest, and ignored his chest hair that tickled her nose. They laid together until the sun began to light up the cloudy sky, and that's when she knew it was time for her to leave. She reluctantly rolled over, and scooped her hospital gown up from the floor. She slipped it on in silence.

"I love you, Rosie." Stephan said genuinely, as he placed a hand on her shoulder from behind.

"I love you too, and I really hope we can do this again. I really do hope . . .

that we do get out of here, and we can have some kind of life." She said as she held his hand in hers, and placed it against her cheek. She turned to look at him, and gave him a long goodbye kiss. "I have to go . . . see you at breakfast." She slipped out of his room just as quietly as she had entered. Stephan went to his door and pulled out the metal rectangle from the strike plate, and allowed the door to silently lock. He went over to his bed, and slid the metal into the hole of his mattress that once held the pills. He thought he may need it again. Rosie didn't know it, but she had given him an important key in their escape. He had been trying to formulate a foolproof plan to get out.

Stephan laid in his bed, and dozed lightly until a nurse opened the door and announced breakfast. He felt exhausted, but that didn't matter because of the night he had. It was worth the tired and euphoric feeling he was feeling. He looked forward to seeing Rosie again, especially after what happened the night before. When he entered the cafeteria, he saw that she was second in line. He hastily got his tray and walked to the table in the corner.

"Good morning, lovely," Stephan said with a beaming smile, "because of you, I just might be nice to Nurse Satan."

"You're off to a good start with the nickname already. You should be flying below the radar. Quit doing things to attract attention to yourself." Rosie advised.

"Well, listen to you. We spend one night together, and I guess that makes you the boss. You sound like a wife."

"Maybe one day," She looked down at her tray and blushed. The comment came out before she could think twice about it. She only meant to think it, not say it out loud.

"I wouldn't mind that." Stephan's reply made her cheeks turn a deeper red. "Whom do you think will be drooling on themselves today?" He said, changing the subject.

"Wanda will probably be proceeding into a control room. Maybe Paul too. Marcus wasn't looking so good. I don't know the story with that Fiona, I know she's bat shit though." She said with pitying tone. "Soon it could be me. I haven't been feeling like myself since yesterday."

"What do you mean?" He asked.

"A little light headed, kinda feel like I'm floating a bit."

"I wish you would stop taking those damn pills."

"I'm not you Stephan. I have always lived my life being safe, and staying out of trouble. Those homes I was in, if you got in trouble, it was bad. So, I just follow the rules I guess."

"I'm not saying for you to advertise that you're not taking the pills." Stephan said heatedly.

"Listen, they could know. Even if I acted like I was doped up, and cheeked my pills . . . what if the time came for them to think I was ready for a control room, and it's an excruciating process. What if the meds are there to take that away?"

"I don't know, I figured we would be gone by then."

"Stephan . . . we are still here, and you haven't gotten any type of plan. It's time to admit that this is what it is, and that this is happening."

"No. I won't admit defeat."

"Then it's going to be one violent shove into reality for you when that time comes." She shook her head disappointedly, and got up to clear her tray. She left Stephan alone at the cafeteria table. It was the first time she walked away from him, and he didn't like it. They had different views on the escape. Rosie felt that she was right to surrender to will of the hospital. Stephan was too headstrong to admit defeat. There was a child bully in his subconscious that was pushing him down, and telling him he was an idiot if he thought any of this would work out to his advantage. It gave him a shred of doubt that seemed to keep him from formulating a decent plan of escape. The demon that followed him whispered its negativity, and gave him panic attacks that woke him in the middle of the night with cold sweats. It was the same fragment of doubt that uttered a small voice, and kept nagging him to give in to the hospital. The voice that quietly beckoned him to become like the rest of the unfortunate souls who happen to pass through the walls of Euphoria Hills Institution. Never to see the light of day outside of a window again.

CHAPTER 10

Time moved slowly at the hospital for every patient. The longer you were there, the more the hours began to feel like days when you were awake. Stephan found sleep hard to come by with all the thoughts running through his head. The red eyes constantly stared him down, and beckoned its orders. He hated being in his room alone, and he wondered how much longer his body and mind would take before everything crashed down around him. The demon was no longer whispering, and it was getting harder for Stephan to ignore. He hoped he would last until he and Rosie were out of the hospital, and safely far away. He could self medicate the demon away as he used to, and the rest Rosie could take care of.

"Say . . . my . . . name!" The demon ordered Stephan again.

"And what do I get in return? Are you going to help us get out of here?" Stephan asked it.

"In one way or another, I could be of some assistance to you." It was no longer whispering now, its voice was low and raspy.

"Not just me . . . Rosie too. She has to get out of all this mess okay."

"Fine! I'll help the woman. You know what you must do though. Now . . . say my name." The shadow's eyes began glowing an intense red that lit up the room like a photography dark room. Stephan was silent and hesitant. He closed his eyes tightly, and let out a long, shaky sigh. When he opened his eyes again, he also opened his mouth to speak the one word the shadow was asking for.

"Orroth." He finally gave in to the being. A slight breeze swept through the room. The temperature rose, and made the room significantly hotter for a few moments.

"Thank you." The being's harsh voice echoed throughout the room. Stephan looked at the demon and saw its red eyes turn into flames. The demon turned into a frightening sight he had never seen before. It had grown three heads.

One head was a bull, the second was a man, and the third was that of a ram. The entity was nude, and sat on a bear. A sparrow hawk accompanied it by sitting upon its wrist. Stephan caught a glimpse of a serpent tail from the back of the being. "Thank you. Now, you'll have the tools to see, and go unseen." Orroth told Stephan in a hoarse voice. He stood in shock by what he was seeing. He wasn't sure if it was real, or if it was a crazy delusion putting on a show. He wasn't sure about what the demon meant by, 'see without being seen' either. The demon reached out and touched Stephan's chest with its large hand. Everywhere its fingertips touched him, burned like a bullet penetrating through him. "I will help you escape this place, but there will be a price to pay in the end." The demon's three heads smiled, and it disappeared into a dark corner. He was suddenly left alone in his room. This was the first time the shadow had left him alone since he arrived at the hospital. It had finally got what it wanted. He had always felt its presence even when he couldn't see it, but now he was completely alone for the first time in years.

When it was time, he made his way to the common room. Rosie wasn't in the room yet, and neither was anyone else. He turned on the television, and found that he had eight channels to choose from. He chose to watch a DIY home renovation show. It was the only interesting thing on. He sat on the couch, and watched the program half-interested while he waited for Rosie. He couldn't shake what happened in his room, and wanted to tell Rosie about it. The minutes felt like hours, and his mind raced. He tried to concentrate on a plan to get them out. The only thing he could think of doing is stealing a key card after assaulting a staff member. He didn't want to attract that much attention. All he could do is keep thinking of a way out. Every time he thought he had devised a decent plan, he ran into a snag and had to start over again. He was caught up in all the 'what ifs' to even come up with a proper escape. He felt by not getting them out as he had promised, that he was letting Rosie down.

Stephan was swamped in his own thoughts, and didn't hear Rosie come in. She flopped down hard on the couch, and broke Stephan out of his trance. He leaned over to say hello, but stopped when he saw her condition. She had fallen back against the couch, and her arms laid limply on her lap. She stared at the television with a vacant expression. He was taken aback at what he saw. This was not the Rosie he had come to know.

"Rosie. Are you okay?" He said reaching for her hand. She quickly snapped to attention, and looked at him sleepily when his hand touched her. What happened in his room would have to wait.

"I took the pills again, and they're really getting to me today." She looked at the television again. "Stephan . . . it's okay. At least we can be together one way or another. Dr. Wagner approved my control room status today. It's only a matter of . . . time before I'll be in one of the control rooms." She said quietly with her speech slightly slurred.

"That's not what I want to hear right now." Stephan found he missed the behavior of Paul. It was part of what he had come to know as normal. He missed Wanda's tapping and Lily's loud, mouthy outbursts. He even missed Marcus' habit. At least they were themselves. He was slowly being surrounded by drones, and the staff at the hospital wanted to make him one.

Sliding feet were heard coming down the hall and toward the common room. Stephan watched as Marcus slowly made his way to a chair, and fell into it. He was in the same state that Paul was in when he fell to the floor the day before. Rosie would be at the point where the two men were by the next day if Stephan didn't act fast. He came to realize that he needed to start acting like Rosie. He couldn't risk anyone catching on that he wasn't taking the medication. The extra pills the patients were taking were undoubtedly responsible for the sluggish behavior. He laid back against the couch, and tried to be fixated on the television like Rosie. He heard Fiona lightly skip on the tiles, and enter the common room. She pranced over to a chair by the couch and sat down.

"Whoa . . . what's with everyone." She politely asked.

"You'll find out soon enough." Stephan told her.

"Whatever do you mean?" She said with the utmost courtesy. She was acting like a woman her age this time.

"What I mean is . . . in a week you're gonna be drooling on yourself and pissing your pants." Stephan said vehemently.

"Well, you seem to be quite coherent." The snob in her began to come out in her tone.

"I'm a special case, sweetheart. I wouldn't go by my example."

"What do you mean . . . you're special?"

"It means that they just haven't found the right meds for me yet."

"Is that what's wrong with everyone here?" She asked. "Are they on the right meds?"

"My, my . . . I thought I was curious." He leaned forward to speak to her. "The drugs are beginning to kick in with them. It will happen to you too. You should know that your time is short when they ask you what your perfect world is. When that happens, you will slowly become a drone like everyone else."

"My perfect world? I already had that. Why would they care here?"

"I don't want to ruin the surprise for ya." Stephan leaned back again, and rested his head against the back of the couch while closing his eyes.

"What surprise? What do you know?" Fiona ordered.

"Let's just say. You're stuck here just like the rest of us."

"My husband is going to come back for me. He and the kids need me. If anyone here is a special case, it's me. I'm not like the rest of you."

"What makes you think you're so damn special? What makes you think you are so fucking sane, and you're not as screwed as everyone else here? Isn't your husband the one that dropped you off in the first place?" He asked, looking at Fiona with anger in his eyes.

"Well, yes." She said, nodding her head and looking away from him.

"I watched him drop you off, just like my wife dropped me off . . . now she's my ex-wife. She came to see me once to tell me she wanted a divorce, and I haven't seen her since. Once you're here, everyone leaves you. Then you're stuck in here and left to rot."

"My husband would never do that to me. He loves me far too much to let me go. We built a lavish life together."

"Oh, you poor, dumb bitch. You really do think you are special, and that he is coming back for you. You thought you were a nine-year-old not too long ago. You're missing some bolts, screws or something in that head of yours." Stephan became silent at the sound of Nurse Adams coming into the room with Wanda.

"Group therapy is about to start." The nurse notified the patients as she turned the television off. Mr. S shuffled into the common room with Paul, and parked his wheelchair with the rest of the group. He took a seat at the front of the room, but tried to avoid the nurse. Nurse Adams stood before the patients, and cleared her throat. "Everyone, lets wish Wanda and Paul, the best of luck. They will be proceeding to a control room later today. We wish you well Wanda and Paul." She took a seat next to Mr. S, and allowed him to take over the therapy session.

"I would like to start with our newest patient, Fiona. How do you feel today?" Mr. S said, beginning the session.

"I'm a little sad. I miss home, and I was just told that once you're here, you don't leave. That frightens me. I'm a little nervous that my husband might forget about me now. I'm also curious about what a control room is."

"Your doctor will get into more about the control rooms with you when the time comes. It sounds like you're feeling a mixture of emotions right now, but you need time to adjust to your new surroundings. It's best to let the dust settle. We don't want you to become overwhelmed. That's why you won't see the doctor right away." Nurse Adams explained to her calmly, answering the question for Mr. S.

"Why is everyone acting like this?" She asked with a quivering voice. The fake way Nurse Adams was acting angered Stephan, and the way she wouldn't give any straight answers made it so he couldn't hold his tongue any longer.

"Here's how it goes." He said sitting forward. He looked into Fiona's big, blue eyes. He could tell she was trying to fight back the tears. "Everyone you have ever loved on the outside . . . gone. You have these sickos, who drug you, and give you vague answers, if none at all. They ask you what your perfect world is, and put you into a fantasy so all us crazies are easily managed, and not a burden to society." He watched tears begin to fall from her eyes that were filled with disbelief.

"This can't be happening. This wasn't supposed to be my life." Fiona began to instantly hyperventilate from anxiety.

"Nice going!" Nurse Adams stood up to lead Fiona from the room to calm her down. "Stevens, get Wanda. We're done in here. Tell an orderly to get Paul." She called over her shoulder. Mr. S obediently gathered his things, and took the patient out of the room. Stephan didn't get a reaction out of the other patients. Rosie had nothing to say either. She sat on the couch, numb to her surroundings. Stephan's world was falling apart yet again, but this time it mattered more than it did before. He had true feelings for Rosie, and cared about what was happening to her. He found himself caring what was happening to other patients as well. He looked at Paul sitting in the wheelchair, drooling on himself just as Mabel and all the others had done. He recalled his attitude towards the process at first, but now things have changed when his Rosie was going to go through the same process. It was no longer funny, and nicknames for drooling patients was no longer a game to him. He knew what was going on in the hospital wasn't right.

What Stephan didn't know is that his speech he gave Fiona put a target on him, and he should have been worried when the whistle wasn't blown on him during the group therapy session. Nurse Adams had a hunch that he wasn't taking his pills already. She knew they would have started their effect on him by now, and he wasn't doing a very good job at faking the symptoms. If Stephan had just kept quiet, he may have been out of the hospital before anyone could do anything about it. As usual, his mouth had gotten him into trouble. Nurse Adams had made up her mind to call Dr. Krochek for an emergency session with Stephan. He had no way of predicting what would happen by the end of the day.

CHAPTER 11

Stephan was sitting on the couch next to a half-conscious Rosie when Nurse Adams came into the common room, and pulled him away.

"The doctor has requested to see you." She said eerily with daggers in her eyes. Stephan immediately felt uneasy. He wasn't scheduled to see Dr. Krochek until the next day. Nurse Adams said nothing, as the pair proceeded down the corridor. The walk to the office seemed to be the longest one he had taken since his arrival. When he was finally inside, he saw there were two orderlies in the room as well.

"What's this all about?" Stephan asked. Before an answer was given, Dr. Krochek barked the order to the men to hold the patient down. "What's this about?" He screamed. The orderlies held Stephan down in a chair as he fought against them. One man held down his upturned arm, and Nurse Adams approached him with a syringe to withdraw blood.

"We will know what this is about in just a moment." Dr. Krochek said as he pulled out a round, flat device from his bottom desk drawer. The nurse quickly and painfully withdrew blood from Stephan's vein. She handed the needle to the doctor who in turn, put it on the device he pulled from his desk. They all waited in silence for a long beep to come from the machine. "Your blood is negative for the medications you're supposed to be taking." The doctor finally announced to everyone with a scowl. Nurse Adams began to sterilize the machine for Dr. Krochek.

"I knew something was going on, doctor. He wasn't acting like someone would be in his phase of the medications." Nurse Adams said arrogantly. The pride in her voice hung in the room alongside Stephan's defeat. She was able to bring him down, and he could see the glee in her eyes. He began to feel sick to his stomach. He was caught, and now he and Rosie were going to be stuck in the hell of a hospital.

"What are you doing with the pills if you aren't taking them?" Dr. Krochek asked with disdain.

"Does that even matter now? You already know enough." Stephan responded in a small voice. He didn't anticipate being caught. If he was going to make a move, it was now or never. He felt the orderlies loosening their grip on him. Stephan saw his opportunity. He ripped his arms away from their hands, and stood up quickly. He grabbed the desk lamp and broke it across the one orderly's face. The other man tried grabbing him from behind, but Stephan reverse head butted him, breaking the man's nose. The orderly was knocked backwards, and blood immediately spurted from his nose. He grabbed the needle that was used to extract his blood, and stabbed Nurse Adams in the shoulder with it. She let out a deafening shriek. Stephan then turned his attention to Dr. Krochek. He began to reach for him, but before he knew it, he saw black. The orderly whom he hit with the lamp gave him a right cross to the jaw, and instantly knocked him out.

When Stephan awoke, he was strapped down to his bed. He had no way of knowing how long he had been like this. He felt very groggy, and it hurt to open his eyes. Stephan glanced around the room and realized everything was fuzzy. He closed his eyes, and fell back asleep until Nurse Adams came into his room to administer a dose of medication by injection.

"What . . . the hell . . . you give me?" He asked. His speech was slurred, and he felt his tongue turn into knots. He could hardly seem to form any words the way he wanted.

"Oh . . . just the medication you weren't taking. Considering you've been out of it for a little over a day, it's had plenty of time to get into your system. You are still able to walk, but you should be careful so you don't fall. These drugs can make you a little woozy. They also tend to kick in a bit faster when they have to be injected." She walked over to the window and opened the curtains to the room. "Today is a big day for our Rosie. You'll be glad to know the doctor signed off on those straps of yours. So, you can come to the group therapy session today." She made her way over to Stephan and let him out of the restraints. "Take your time getting up, but then again you might want to hurry . . . so you can have a longer goodbye." Without explaining any further, Nurse Adams left the room. Stephan struggled to sit upright. He placed his slippered feet on the floor. His body felt limp and weak. When he finally managed to stand, all he could take were small, clumsy steps toward the door. He went into the hallway and stopped. The bright lights made his eyes water excessively at first.

'A longer goodbye? What does she mean by that?' Stephan zoned out, and his mind became blank like a whiteboard. It took him a minute to snap out of a daydream of nothingness, and realize that he wanted to go to the common room. He saw the shadow with the red eyes in the corner by the nurses station, and Stephan shakily raised his left hand and flipped it off. He slowly walked to the doorway of the common room, and leaned into it to glance inside. Fiona was sitting in a chair, and there was a new patient sitting where Paul used to sit. He made his way to his usual spot on the couch and allowed himself to sink to the back. He began to space out yet again, and the rest of the world around him grew silent. He didn't think or speak. He stared into void until his attention was aroused by the shrill voice of Nurse Adams. She brought Rosie into the common room in a wheelchair.

"Look, it's your friend Stephan." The nurse gave a glare of delighted evil to him. She was enjoying every moment of his defeat. She was able to subdue, in her opinion, the worst patient in history. He had lost the battle. There would be no escape from the hell that surrounded him. He waited for Nurse Adams to leave the room before he spoke to Rosie.

"I'm . . . sssoo . . . sssorry." He slurred to her, but she paid no attention to him. She stared at the floor and allowed the drool to fall from her mouth. She had the same look in her eyes as all the others did before her. Stephan gathered his senses that remained, and realized what was happening. He let the tears fall, and looked at Rosie. "I let . . . usss . . . down." He awkwardly reached for her hand, and held onto it as he drifted away again. He stayed this way until Nurse Adams and Mr. S walked into the room and announced the beginning of group therapy. The nurse walked over to him and removed his hand from Rosie's.

"Contact like that between patients is not appropriate." She told him coldly. "Well, our group has dwindled considerably. We are expecting new intakes though . . . so Fiona, Tim, you won't be by yourselves for long. Rosie is proceeding to a control room later today. Let's all wish her well."

"NO!" Stephan bellowed.

"I'm afraid so, and there isn't anything you can do about it." She sneered.

Stephan lacked the will to respond to her snide comment. He closed his eyes, and did the easiest thing for him at that moment. That was to tune everything and everyone out. He heard Nurse Adams announce the end of group. He left his trance, and gathered all his strength to sit forward.

"Good . . . bye, Row Zee. I'm ssorry." He said as he shakily reached for her hand one last time. The nurse wheeled her out of the room quickly when she saw his attempt at affection. Stephan stared at the doorway even after she was gone. He knew he wouldn't see her again. His plans for any future were foiled. He felt hot tears stream down the side of his face again.

"O . . . M . . . G! That was like . . . the most heart wrenching sight I have ever witnessed!" Fiona spouted. "Were you two . . . like an item? Separating lovers is just . . . sooo . . . wrong. They tried taking me away from my boyfriend, the love of my life, but he's going to bust me out . . . don't tell them that!" Fiona kept going on with her sixteen-year-old rambling, and Stephan let the drugs take over his mind and drown her out. He no longer dwelled on the harsh reality of the way everything was going. He was seeing nothing, and had nothing to lose anymore. He sat, unmoving on the couch until he was snapped back into reality, and instructed to go to his room. He sat on his bed and stared out of his window until he was told to go to dinner. Stephan sat without Rosie, and stared at his food. He lacked any appetite, and seemed to have lost the coordination necessary to maneuver the utensils. He continued to sit and stare, and waited for his turn to be placed into one of the control rooms. He didn't care to feel any emotions about anything. He was numb to most of his being, and was losing his self awareness. Stephan went straight to his room after dinner and lie in his bed. He didn't think about Rosie anymore, but he did see the shadow with the red eyes occasionally. It would whisper to him softly, but he didn't feel it's presence as strongly as he once had. He found it difficult to understand the words it was speaking to him. Time passed, and Nurse Adams came into his room and turned on the lights. She had a syringe with her.

"Time for night meds. I thought I'd personally give yours to you before I left for the night." He allowed her to roughly grab his arm, and inject the medicine into his system. "You're going to be ready for a control room in a day or two. All I have to say is . . . good riddance. I'll be happier with you gone." She turned off the lights and slammed the door on Stephan. The medication he was given helped him quickly drift into a deep and dreamless sleep.

Meanwhile in Control Room 1, Rosie had been put under, and was already living in her perfect world. She neglected to tell Stephan some of the details of her perfect world. He was a stay at home dad to their two children while she worked.

"Carmichael, you need to wake up." A male voice shouted. Rosie shot up from the bunk she was napping on.

"What is it?"

"The target has been acquired." The man said with a smile.

"Excellent." Rosie stood up and straightened her suit. She followed the man through the door. They went down a narrow corridor that led to a room with a large control panel. Rosie took the seat behind the main control panel and began to press a series of buttons. "Missiles are locked on the target." She paused, flipped up a cover that revealed a red trigger. "Ready to fire." Rosie waited for her command. The man came up behind her and sighed.

"Fire." He quietly told her. Without hesitation she squeezed the trigger, and two missiles were released from her submarine. They penetrated a straight, rapid line through the water, and toward the target.

"Closing in on target in 3 . . . 2 . . . 1, the target has been destroyed, sir." Rosie stated, and she began the journey back home. The man threw down fifty thousand dollars in front of Rosie.

"Here's the other half, as we agreed. I can afford it now with the ex-wife out of the picture."

"Good thing you paid up, I wouldn't want to have to kill you too." Rosie smiled at the man. He laughed nervously, and headed back to his cabin. Once Rosie docked the submarine, she looked at the man. "You never met me and the number you had, you will never be able to call again. Goodbye Mr. Sorin." At that, Rosie and the man made their final departure, never to speak of what happened. Rosie was anxious to make it home to her husband and children after being away on a job for three days. She pulled up to their three story Victorian style home, and pulled her black McLaren 570GT into the garage. She made her way into the house, and was welcomed by two excited children and her adoring husband, Stephan.

"How was work, darling? It's great to finally have you home!" He said. Her son and daughter bounced at her feet, and chattered excitedly at the same time. They pulled at her clothes, and mauled her before she could get the shoes off of her feet.

"Work was fine. I have some time off now. I made a lot of money with this job." Rosie smiled at Stephan, and showed him one hundred thousand dollars in cash that she had stowed in her purse. His mouth dropped open and began to form into a smile.

"Mommy, what do you do?" Rosie's son asked.

"Your mommy is a wonderful artist. The reason she has to go away for a few days sometimes . . . is because she is trying to sell her art." Stephan explained.

"I don't ever see mommy painting."

"That's because your mommy's art . . . is a different kind of art. Art isn't always painting and sculpting."

"I don't get it daddy. Art is painting, drawing, and stuff like that. I never see mommy do any of that." Their daughter argued.

"Mommy, maybe you can take me on one of your trips. I want to see your art." The little boy looked at his mother with his big brown eyes expectantly.

"When you're a little older, sweetheart." Rosie managed to say. She gave Stephan a look like she was going to let him have it later. "Right now, I think it's about that time to get pajamas on, and get into bed." Both of the children groaned, and reluctantly made their way up the stairs in front of their parents. Stephan and Rosie tucked their children in, and went downstairs into their kitchen. Stephan treated himself to two fingers of whiskey, and Rosie poured herself a glass of wine. She stared at him in silence and shook her head.

"What?" He asked.

"An artist? Really?" Rosie rolled her eyes.

"I think what you do is art. Assassin . . . artist . . . either way you're making something beautiful."

"Stephan, I destroy things, I take lives. Artists are creators."

"The people you are doing away with, were being pieces of shit. So it's art, my dear, you are creating a better world." Stephan rationalized. "I love you for that."

Stephan was jerked awake by the soft spoken, red-haired nurse calling him to breakfast. He pushed himself to slowly make it out of bed and to the bathroom. When he got to the cafeteria, he didn't bother to get a tray. He sat at the table in the corner by himself, and waited for breakfast to be over. His mind was trapped in a fog. He didn't feel like doing anything except lie in his bed. Instead of doing that, he made his way to the common room after the morning meal where he saw Fiona sitting by herself.

"Hello again." She said with a half smile. Stephan just groggily glanced at her, and shrugged his shoulders. He managed to make a small moan in the back of his throat as he sat down on the couch. Fiona stared at him with bewilderment. "I thought you were immune to what was happening to everyone else." She added. Stephan heard what she said, and with a quavering hand he managed to stick his middle finger up at her. He debated on leaving. He didn't want to hear Fiona talking, but decided it was just as easy to fall away from reality in his own head. After all, he never knew which Fiona he was going to get. Nine years old, sixteen years old or the uppity snob. He wasn't quite sure how many personalities lived inside her. She was easy to tune out. The nurse who woke him up for breakfast came into the common room to retrieve Stephan for his morning dose.

"Can you walk?" She asked blandly. Stephan struggled to sit forward, but rolled off of the couch and onto the floor like Paul had done. "I'll get a wheelchair." The nurse sighed. She left quickly and wasn't gone long before she was back with the chair. She was accompanied by an orderly to assist her in lifting Stephan into the wheelchair. Once he sat, it was over. From here, he would turn into what Rosie and all the others had become. He had witnessed the devastation first hand, but he was too tired and drugged to care. He didn't think about Rosie anymore. He didn't think about his ex-wife or how he lost everything. The nurse took him to a medicine supply room where the injection was ready. She cleaned his arm and gave him the medication.

"You know, it's all going to be over soon. It should be pretty easy for you here on out." She said empathetically. The nurse took Stephan to his room, and placed his chair in front of the window. She opened his curtains. "At least you have a view." She said before she stepped out of the room. He was left there alone until he was taken to see Dr. Krochek. He saw the green truck, but didn't care. There was another patient with a staff member smoking a cigarette, but Stephan was too numb to pay attention or give any of it a second thought. The nurse could have parked him in front of a blank wall, and it wouldn't have made a difference to him.

Inside the doctor's office, Stephan was wheeled up to his desk. He knew the doctor was talking, but his words melted together, and didn't make any sense to him. He found it hard to concentrate, but managed to hear the words control room approval out of all the jumbled conversation. Before he knew it, he was back in his room. He didn't remember the walk back from Dr. Krochek's office, nor did he know how long he had been back in his room staring out of his window. He drifted in and out of a state of consciousness. Stephan didn't go to the cafeteria anymore. He waited patiently for the inevitable end. He heard someone come into his room, and felt them grab a hold of the wheelchair. They took him to the common room. It was to be Stephan's last group therapy session. What he couldn't understand the doctor saying earlier was that Stephan was approved for a control room, and he would proceed early the following morning. A sober person would worry about this, considering everything they have to do to prepare a patient. Fortunately for Stephan, he would be asleep for the whole process. He wouldn't know what was happening until he was in his perfect world with Rosie. He would be living as if they were never in the hospital. He wouldn't remember how his wife had betrayed him. It would just be simple bliss for him. He was barely aware of the orderly that moved him from the wheelchair to his bed. He never felt his nightly injection going into his arm. Stephan finally said goodbye to the last bit of reality that existed for him.

CHAPTER 12

The next morning Nurse Adams entered Stephan's room and gave him another injection. Dr. Montgomery began to feed a silicone tube into Stephan's nose. This would be connected to a polymeric formula that would provide fat, protein and carbohydrates while he was sedated. A nurse put on gloves, and began the process for Stephan's catheter. Dr. Krochek and Nurse Adams were having a hushed discussion in the corner. The nurse nodded in agreement, and the doctor left to set up the machine in the control room. Stephan had four electrodes placed to the left side of his chest, and four more on each side of his head. An orderly released the brakes on his bed, and pushed him out of the room. They began going towards the double doors that Stephan went through many times before to see Dr. Krochek. The orderly pushed him to the second set of doors at the end of the hallway. When you were up close, you could see a sign on the door that read CONTROL ROOMS. Nurse Adams stopped the orderly at the foot of the bed.

"I have it from here." She told him. The man nodded, and turned to go the other way. She waited for the orderly to be a safe distance away before she went to the head of the bed, and looked down at the sedated Stephan. "For someone who had so much fight in him, you sure do look weak and pathetic now. You're going to be put into a diaper like a helpless child, and you and that woman will never see each other again. I knew all about you two. I saw you on the cameras." She began pushing the bed slowly. "I don't know why I'm even wasting my time talking to you. You didn't listen when you were conscious . . ." Her voice trailed off as they approached a door that read CONTROL ROOM 3. She pushed the bed inside where Dr. Krochek was waiting. Inside the room there were nine other patients hooked up to machines that gave them views of an alternate reality. Stephan was wheeled to the very end, and Nurse Adams put the brakes on the bed. She grabbed wires, and began to connect them to the electrodes that were attached to him. She hooked the ones from his chest up to a monitor for his heart, and the ones from his head up to a machine to measure his brain activity. She connected the silicone hose hanging out of his nostril to a bag, and proceeded to lift his hospital gown to put a disposable brief on him. The last thing she did was connect his catheter to a bag to collect his urine, and hung the bag under his bed. Dr. Krochek placed a large device attached to an mechanical arm over Stephan's head. Metal plates automatically came from the machine after a button was pushed, and suctioned themselves tightly to the sides of his head. Rubber brackets forced his eyes to stay open while little tubes delivered drops of artificial tears on a timed schedule to keep his eyes lubricated. Ahead of him, a hologram screen moved closer to his eyes. Dr. Krochek set up what he needed to on the computers. Stephan was now ready to begin to live in his perfect world. As far as Nurse Adams and Dr. Krochek were concerned, Stephan was another burden to society that had been dealt with accordingly. In their opinion, they deserved a pat on the back for a job well done.

Life at the hospital continued. More patients came in, and were put into a nocturnal state for the experiment. Dr. Krochek welcomed a class of medical students into the hospital to show them how the mentally ill were dealt with and diagnosed. They all crowded into Stephan's control room.

"This is patient 0146982007. She is thirty-six years old, and her physical health is good. Her diagnosis is Schizophrenia with homicidal tendencies and suicidal behavior, such as self mutilation. We have set up a world for her where she can be with her husband and children, and not be a danger to society or herself." The doctor moved to the man next to Stephan and grabbed his tablet. "This is patient 0099490721. He is forty two years old with a mild heart condition. He suffers from severe depression and he has attempted suicide on many different occasions after the loss of his wife in a head on automobile collision. He was also diagnosed with Post Traumatic Stress Disorder due to the fact he was in the car with them and saw them die. He also has homicidal tendencies towards the other driver." He put the tablet back at the foot of the man's bed and turned to address the students. "So, you see, we are doing a service here at Euphoria Hills Institution. These people are given adequate care for their conditions. Someday you could be part of this technology that is taking the medical field by storm. This is cutting edge technology that is the future, and you are all the future." The students listened intently as Dr. Krochek finished his inspirational speech, and they departed from the room.

Stephan awoke in a large, comfortable bed with sheets that smelled like fresh lavender. He heard dishes clinking together downstairs. He smiled and stretched before he sat up. He put his feet into monogrammed slippers, and walked into a large master bathroom. It had a large Jacuzzi tub and two sinks that was accompanied by a large, well-lit mirror. There was a private stall with a large oak door for the toilet. When Stephan finished in the bathroom, he made his way down a set of curved stairs. He neared the sound of pots and pans banging together. He found himself in a large kitchen with granite counter tops and stainless steel appliances. Rosie was on the other side of an island counter top with her back turned to Stephan. Her hair was pulled up neatly into a ponytail. She didn't hear Stephan enter the kitchen because she was busy, vigorously scrubbing a pan with a scouring pad.

"Good morning, darling." Stephan announced his presence and startled her. She dropped the pan into the sink, and foamy bubbles flew onto the dark counter top.

"Honey! You're awake! I was hoping to give you breakfast in bed!" She smiled sweetly at him. She loved the way his dark hair looked in the morning. The two inches of messy, wavy tangles went everywhere, and were a sure sign of a good night's rest.

"That's okay. We can eat out on the porch together." He told her with a bright smile. Rosie agreed, and left the pan she was scrubbing to join

Stephan on the back porch. She brought their breakfast out on a serving tray, and set it on a coffee table in front of a white wicker couch. A beautiful garden grew in the backyard, and the scent of lilacs filled the air. The swinging door of the enclosed porch led to a set of concrete stairs. At the bottom, was a stone path to a swing surrounded by lilies. There was trellis with climbing roses and ivy growing around it. Rosie worked hard to maintain her garden. It was complete and total bliss for the couple. Stephan worked as a well-read professor who wasn't afraid to challenge logic, and was respected among his colleagues. He had received awards for his many findings and written words. He could afford to give his wife anything she desired. She had the luxury and humility to be a homemaker. Rosie wasn't the type to hire someone to clean up their mess or have absurd demands.

"It's going to be a beautiful day." Rosie gave a sigh of contentment as she reached for a cup of tea.

"I know it is. Why shouldn't it be after an amazing night?" Stephan looked at Rosie, and winked with a sideways grin. He turned his gaze to the rounded hills in the distance.

"I have news for you." She said softly. He was looking at the view of the hills, and didn't look away to respond to her.

"What's that, my dear?" Stephan was enjoying a warm breeze as he slowly ate his breakfast, and sipped his hot tea.

"I'm pregnant." This caused Stephan to stop chewing his English muffin, and jerk his head toward her. After a slight moment of silence, he finally managed to find his words.

"Really?" He allowed the news set in, and a huge smile swept across his face. Rosie pulled a positive pregnancy test from her apron pocket, and handed it to Stephan. "Wow! I'm going to be a father . . . a daddy! Honey! You've made me the happiest man on the planet! In the universe!" He stood up and took her hand, and pulled her up to him. "I hope it's a boy."

"A little Stephan Jr." Rosie said with a smile.

"Then we could try for a girl next, and he could protect his little sister."

"How about we have this one first, Casanova." Rosie laughed. "So what do you want to do today?"

"Well, I have office hours from three to six. Those ungrateful bastards are lucky to get that on a Saturday, but other than that . . . I'm yours. We have to tell Bill! He has been wanting us to have a child for so long."

"Okay, we can tell Bill." Rosie smiled at Stephan again, and stared deeply into his eyes.

"Do you think it's to soon to look for a crib, and some stuff like that?" She asked brightly.

"Absolutely not. Let me hop in the shower really quick, and I'll be ready.

We can stop and tell Bill the good news on the way."

"Okay, I'll go change." She said excitedly, already untying her apron from around her waist. From this moment on, their lives were going to be different.

Stephan met Rosie downstairs after a quick, steamy shower. She had the car keys and her purse ready. They went through the garage door, and got into the black, twentieth century '69 Dodge Charger. The 440 fuel injected engine roared to life. He revved the engine and smiled at the sound of the turbo. He had the perfect wife, house, job and car. Stephan had the perfect life. They pulled out of the driveway, and made their way towards town to shop for the new addition to their family.

"We should consider buying a family oriented vehicle. I'm not saying you should get rid of the Dodge . . . but let's get something else that would be better for a baby." Rosie said as they rolled down their private lane.

"I agree. You know I could never get rid of Cordelia though. She is the only girl I'm allowed to have on the side." Stephan said jokingly.

"You couldn't handle another woman." She poked back.

"You're probably right. You're enough of a woman for me." He reached over to hold her hand in his, and she wove her fingers into his. Five minutes down the road, they pulled into a driveway, and Stephan cut the engine. A man was sitting in a white rocking chair on his porch, and sipping a cup of coffee. "Bill!

How are you?" Stephan shouted from the car window. The bull that fed on hay nearby in the field by his barn didn't seem phased by the loud car that pulled into the driveway. Bill was tall with black hair. He had the most mesmerizing, dark eyes anyone has ever seen on a human being. His voice was hoarse, and he had a dominant personality. Stephan and Bill had the same type of finesse and sarcasm, which is why they got along well. "Bill, I finally managed to do it. Rosie is going to have my baby."

"Congratulations! That's great to hear you two! It's about time." Bill said in a raspy voice. He stepped down from the porch and came to the driver side window of Stephan and Rosie's car. A fenced in ram beat its horns against the fence in the side of Bill's yard. "Where are you two headed on this beautiful morning?" He asked, ignoring his pet.

"Just going to pick out some baby stuff." Rosie interjected with glowing pride.

"Never too soon to start." He said, giving Rosie a wink. "How's the job going?" He asked, shifting his attention back to Stephan.

"Going good. Great in fact. Things have finally started to slow down too.

Just in time if you ask me." Stephan reached over, and touched Rosie's stomach.

"Looks as if your farm is doing well."

"Yeah, I've had a good crop this year, so far. My farm is small, but it flourishes." Bill looked around at his property. "Well, God Bless you both, and congratulations, again." Bill said with a wide, toothy smile before he sent them on their way. Stephan started the car, put it in drive, and pulled away from Bill's farm.

"I love you baby." She said as she relaxed against the back of the seat.

"I love you too darling." He said, reaching over and giving her hand a slight squeeze. They both relaxed on the ten minute commute to their quaint little town.

It had been six months since Stephan was put into a control room. The hospital still ran like clockwork, and practiced their unorthodox methods. The machines that the patients were connected to were still in the experimental stages, and were sometimes apt to fail.

". . .if the state ever finds out about this . . . the hospital will be shut down, and everything we've worked for will have been for nothing." A male voice was heard by patient 0099490721 as he slipped out of his deep sleep, and his equipment began to fail. An obnoxious alarm was heard to signal that this had happened. The patient groaned, and began to move around. The man made his way over to a cabinet. He retrieved a syringe and a sedative to inject into the patient. The nurse he was talking to, aided the man in putting the waking patient back to sleep. She connected a fresh bag of medicine, and reset the equipment. "Who is he, doctor?" She asked.

"How could I forget Paul? He lost his wife and child in a drunk driving accident, and he tried to kill himself. He was sent here as a suicide risk. He is also the twin brother of our very own Dr. Montgomery. Can't you see the resemblance? Monty wanted him here so he could watch him more closely. He cares a lot about his brother. We try to take special care of him." He explained.

"How is our . . . other . . . situations?"

"The patient has been cremated, and her COD is due to an allergic reaction to medication." The woman responded quietly.

"Has the coroner signed off on it?"

"Yes, doctor."

"Excellent." He cleared his throat. "It would seem everything has been dealt with and everything is in order." The nurse headed toward the door to exit the room. "Oh, Nurse!"

"Yes sir." She turned around to face him.

"You're sure we don't have any loose ends . . . correct?"

"I'm almost . . . ninety-nine percent positive, doctor."

"Hmm, maybe I'll just check with Nurse Adams to be absolutely sure. I want to be one hundred and ten percent sure on this matter. I'm sure you understand." The doctor waved the nurse along, and continued to contemplate in the quiet room. Nothing like this had ever happened in the history of the hospitals existence. None of the staff was sure of what to make of what had happened. No one was sure how the patient had a way to make it happen, and most of all, who was it with? Either way, it's what caused her death. It's what could bring the demise of the hospital if the public ever found out about the terrible cover up. Some of the staff was stressed out about the horrible drama unfolding. Others were in storm prep mode for the coming weather. None of the patients knew that one of them had died.

CHAPTER 13

The winter of 2087 officially started when six inches of snow fell overnight in early January. However, the worst was yet to come. According to the weather man, a snow storm that would cause power outages was on its way. It would have white outs accompanied with below freezing temperatures. Fifty to sixty-five-mile an hour gusts of wind were expected. Everyone was being advised to stock up on what they could ahead of time, and to stay indoors. Luckily, the hospital had an old generator that ran on propane that would get them through the storm. They haven't had to use it in years, because a storm like this hasn't been seen since Super Storm Brandon of 2072.

Pete Majors, the hospital's maintenance man, went into town to gather provisions such as fuel, food and other things. Everyone was in a frenzy in town trying to get last minute supplies. Cases of water, nonperishable food, medical supplies, and blankets were flying off of the shelves. The hospital already had a plentiful food and water supply. Pete was concerned about getting fuel to keep the generator going. He couldn't risk the hospital losing power. Pete pulled up to the propane dealer and went inside. He set up an emergency delivery to have the one thousand-gallon propane tank filled. He needed the tank of propane to keep the 150 kW, 120/240 volt unit running when the power went out. He wanted to make sure they had enough to wait out the storm. When he completed the order, Pete headed back to the hospital. The truck bounced up the driveway that led behind the hospital. Pete pulled up to a door and cut the truck's engine. He stepped out and looked at the ominous sky. It sent a chill up his spine, but deep down he knew it wasn't only the weather that gave him the creeping feeling. He went to a door in the back of the building and pulled out a key ring to unlock it. Once Pete was inside, he heard the furnace kick on. He inspected the generator while he waited for the propane delivery to come. Suddenly, there was a loud bang on the basement door. This made Pete jump out of his skin. He walked over to the door and cracked it open. He breathed a sigh of relief when he saw it was the man delivering the propane. He swung the door open the rest of the way and stepped outside to greet the delivery man. The two men conducted their business. Pete bid the man farewell when he signed a tablet with a stylus for the delivery to be charged to the hospital. He hastily made his way back inside. He started the generator, and it roared to life without hesitation. This made Pete smile to himself, because it meant he wasn't going to have to mess around with repairs. When he was finished with the generator, he went to a room he made for himself in the back corner. He wasn't sure what the room was used for before it was his. He made it his own and didn't dwell on the history of what it was used for prior.

Pete used an old hospital bed in a room in the corner of the basement. He adopted old furniture the hospital was throwing away. He fixed it and used it to furnish his room. He had a dresser, a couple bookcases and a desk. He managed to acquire a small hologram television and an Insta-heater, even though they were recalled for the lasers being too dangerous. Everyone went back to using a microwave when a mistake in manufacturing had accidently cut someone's hand off at the wrist by a heat laser when they tried to retrieve their food. He was hoping to get a refrigerator soon, and eventually an electric portable stove.

The only staff aware that Pete lived on the grounds was Nurse Adams and Dr. Krochek. The basement had an old, working bathroom that included a shower. He had everything he needed. He lived off of canned goods and crackers. He was happy living this way, and because of Pete, the hospital was ready to survive the storm 2087.

Night came swiftly, and it was time for shift change. The nurse and the orderly who enjoyed each others company was working again. After making a good impression for a half hour, they made their way to their usual spot for what they planned to do with one another. Their spot happened to be Control Room 3. The nurse who liked her crossword puzzles was sitting at the desk trying to figure out seven across, and the other orderly found some cartoons to watch on the television. He would be entertained for quite some time. Everything was normal tonight, or so it would seem.

The young nurse and orderly entered into Control Room 3. Ten people, covered in sheets and hooked up to machines, lie still in a neat row. Beeping heart monitors and oxygen pumping could be heard. The blue LED lights made things a bit harder to see.

"Why do you always wanna do it in here?" The orderly asked the nurse with a slight shiver. "I mean . . . your body is bangin' and your face is beautiful, but this shit is just creepy, yo!" A sadistic smile spread across her face, and she walked over to the patient in the third bed.

"You see this guy right here?" She asked looking at the man, deep in his slumber in the bed.

"Yeah . . . I see him . . . what about him?" He said curtly, gesturing with his hands while looking up at the ceiling.

"Before he was put under, he tried to rape me. Full on attacked me . . . had to be sedated and strapped until it was his time to come in here. He's a real piece of shit." She paused and hovered over the man. "What's your perfect world . . . a rape-fest, you sick fuck?" She started to undo the buttons on her white nurse's blouse over his sleeping body. "Bet you wish you could touch these, asshole." She whispered sensually. She hovered over his forehead. Her breasts grazed his blond hair.

"That just kinda makes it even more fucked up that you want to do it in here with him being in here, and that you're doing that." The orderly pointed out uneasily. The nurse slowly walked over to him, unbuttoning her blouse the rest of the way, revealing the rest of her black lacy bra.

"I do it because he wishes he could have had this, but I want to drive him crazy by giving it to you. Now shut the fuck up, and quit over analyzing it." She took her top off and hopped up on the side of the last bed . . . Stephan's bed. The nurse hiked up her skirt, and motioned for the orderly to, 'come here'.

"No panties again . . . You're such a bad girl, but you know just how I like it." He grunted, forgetting about the conversation they were having. The orderly was too caught up in the moment with the nurse, that he didn't realize he was stepping on a tube. The tube in which delivered Stephan's medicine that kept him happily sedated. It was being pinched off, and with every thrust he gave the nurse, it became weaker. The tube eventually snapped in two, and allowed the medicine to run onto the floor instead of into Stephan's vein. Stephan would only remain sedated for an hour or two longer before he awoke feeling like the morning after his twenty first birthday. The nurse and orderly didn't realize what they had done, and left the control room when they were finished, and headed back to the unit.

"Hey! Hey! You! Where the hell have you two been?" The young orderly and nurse were stopped suddenly, and surprised at what they saw. Nurse Adams was at the nurses station, and looked highly disgruntled at the slacking that was going on with the shift. The other nurse and orderly were white faced and wide eyed, but didn't say a word. "Never mind that, we need to make sure that generator kicks on as soon as we lose power."

"I thought you went home, Nurse Adams." The young nurse squeaked.

"I've been in Dr. Krochek's office. He's still here too. So if any of you feel like messing around anymore, I suggest you get that idea out of your heads." She said coldly, narrowing her eyes at each staff member. Just as she said that, the wind howled and blew against the building and made the lights flicker. "Get the battery powered radio and reserve batteries for it. We also need flashlights." Nurse Adams ordered. Everyone scrambled all at once to find something useful to do.

Downstairs in the basement, Pete was preparing the generator to automatically turn on when the power went off. The power would have to be off for thirty seconds before it would kick on. That was the best he could do. The hospital wouldn't invest in a better generator. They opted for the thirty thousand dollar generator to save money, instead of the eighty five-thousand dollar one, which would have had no lag time at all. Pete watched the snow blow in under the gap of the door going to the outside. He listened to the wind howl, and tried to guess which ones were going to make the lights flicker. One angry blast came and knocked the power out long enough for the generator to kick on momentarily after the thirty seconds of waiting. The lights flickered back on, and the generator shut off again two minutes later when the power came back. Pete was grateful for the automatic switch, but he knew it was still going to be a long night.

The raging winds that caused power loss went on for an hour and half. The nurses assumed everything was all right, because the patients were drugged even if the machines didn't work for a moment. The patients would stay asleep. Dr. Krochek stayed in his office and was calling his wife. He reassured her that he was needed at the hospital tonight in case anything happened with the patients. In Control Room 3, Stephan was slowly coming out of his slumber. His machine was stuck to his head, but he was becoming aware that it wasn't real. His conscious mind was returning to him, and his first initial thought was that he had been abducted.

"Aliens!" He shrieked raspily when he reached up and felt the tube taped to his face that went into his nose. He saw a white tube that dropped a lubricating drop in his eye every five seconds. He wasn't able to blink because of the rubber brackets that pressed onto his eyelids. Then his memory quickly began to trickle back into his mind and he quieted himself. He remembered his last visit to Dr. Krochek's office, and Rosie.

'For the love of God! I've been given a second chance. I can't waste it by losing my shit now. I have to get to Rosie.' Stephan gave himself a small pep talk, and took some deep breaths. The brackets keeping his eyes open, and the tube in his nose is what bothered him the most. He wanted to blink, but no matter how hard he tried, the brackets pressed his eyelids open. The lights flickered out, and suddenly the machine let go of his head completely. The room was dark except the emergency light on the fire alarm. He pushed the contraption away as far as he could from him with its mechanical arm, and just lie there and thought about his next move. He grabbed the electrodes and started pulling them off of his chest and head. The lights suddenly flickered back on, but he continued to pull out the IV in his arm. He removed everything that they were using to keep track of him while he was in his nocturnal state. He peeled the tape from his face and slowly started to pull the tube out of his nose. He breathed hard through his teeth as he did this and fought the sensation to sneeze.

"Aw, shit on me!" Stephan said out loud when he saw the catheter coming out of the diaper. He stood up from the bed on wobbly legs, and took the diaper off to get a better look at the tube coming out of the tip of his manhood. "How the fuck can I get this bitch out?" He gave it a slight tug, and he growled with discontentment. Stephan looked around the room and saw a cart in the corner. He began to clumsily walk toward it, but was stopped dead in his tracks. The short catheter hose pulled him back, and he let out a short shriek of pain. He realized it was attached to a bag under the bed. He mumbled profanities under his breath, grabbed the bag and carried it with him to the cart. He finally found a scalpel in a drawer and cut the hose leaving two inches of catheter hose hanging out of the tip. *'Rosie will get the joke.'* He laughed to himself. He tied up the hospital gown in the back and found another gown to wear over that to cover the semi-open back of him. He found a tablet with his information on it in a slot at the end of the bed he was in, and he decided to take it. He placed the scalpel in a pocket, and opened the door to exit Control Room 3. Stephan found himself in the dimly lit hallway. His legs were a little shaky, but he wasn't going to let that stop him now. He turned toward the windowless double doors. His first order of business was to get to Krochek's office and find out where Rosie was. He needed to erase the fact that they were here by finding any other copies of their information. To go through these double doors from this side, no key card was needed. They led into the hallway of the doctor's offices, where he had been many times before. Just as Stephan came into the hallway, he saw Krochek disappear into his office. He held his breath and thankfully, he didn't notice the awakened patient. So he decided to take advantage of the opportunity that the doctor was alone in his office. Stephan crept up to Dr. Krochek's door and ducked out of sight where the camera had no way of seeing him, no matter which direction it looked in. He waited there, wondering what he would do once he had the man in front of him, and he had the upper hand. Did he want to kill him? He sat there thinking about what his move was going to be once he persuaded the doctor to open the door. Stephan decided that he actually wanted to kill the family of Dr. Krochek, so he knew what it was like to lose everything, and be powerless to stop it. Did he even have a family? What woman would marry someone so dry? Whom could he go after that meant something to the doctor? Maybe Krochek would be better off dead . . . maybe he would have a personality in the afterlife. Stephan decided his goal was to get the patient information for him and Rosie. Then, he would probably tie the doctor to a chair and have his twisted versions of fun for a moment before he moved along. He pressed the button and waited. *'There's no turning back now!'* He thought to himself.

"Hello?" The camera's movement could be heard searching for the person who pressed the button. Dr. Krochek was quick to dismiss the situation, and hung up on the intercom, but never came to the door. Stephan did it again. He hit the white button, and this time he traded places with the scalpel and tablet. "Hello? Nurse Adams? Is that you?" A long pause. "This fucking storm, I swear." The intercom hung up again. Stephan bit his lip to stifle his laughter, because this was starting to get hilarious for him. He reached up and rang the bell again.

"MOTHER FUCKER!" He heard an angry, muffled voice from behind the door. Stephan felt his eyes widen, this was it. He was coming . . . he had won! The office door clicked open. As it swung open, Stephan stood up, and whirled around quickly. He held the scalpel to Dr. Krochek's throat. He pushed him inside the office and kicked the door closed behind him.

"Why, hello Doctor! Remember me?"

CHAPTER 14

"All I'm picking up on the radio is static." The young nurse said, annoyed and frustrated. "This thing is ancient."

"It's because you're not doing it right. You have to move this thing around." The young orderly began adjusting the long antennae.

"You . . . are . . . so . . . fucking . . . stupid. You think you know everything." She rolled her eyes and walked away.

"At least I'm trying, which is more than what your bitchy ass is doing!" The orderly yelled after her. He rolled his eyes at her and flipped her off behind her back.

"Why don't you two just get married, and be done with it already?" The older nurse said to him.

"What do you know about anything besides crossword puzzles and sleeping?" The young orderly responded snidely.

"I worked here long enough to see some shit, and I know you two sneak off to do the nasty when you work together. If you ever wanna learn anything . . . you'd be smart to come around and listen to some words of wisdom."

"You're fucking weird. You know that? Fuck this radio, and this stupid storm." The orderly left the nurses station in a huff, and went to find the young nurse to apologize to her.

The generator had been permanently running for the last two hours. The wind blew a tree into the power lines that fed the hospital. Pete had been doing his job, and making sure it didn't need any maintenance. Nurse Adams was taking care of a loose end. A patient had died, and on behalf of Dr. Krochek she was making sure all details were in order. The doctor was the busiest of all the staff at the hospital. Stephan had a scalpel against his throat and had him trapped in his office. Dr. Krochek had no way of getting help.

"Well, do ya? Do ya remember doc?" Stephan asked.

"How could I forget . . ." Dr. Krochek trembled and swallowed hard. Stephan pulled the scalpel away from his throat, and put his arm around the doctor's shoulders.

"Let's play a game. I want to be the doctor, and you can be the patient." Stephan said excitedly as he led Dr. Krochek over to the chair where he once sat in front of the desk. He pushed the doctor down into it. "Now don't make a run for it or I'll have to throw this scalpel into your spine." He said right in the doctor's face with a twisted smile. Dr. Krochek saw nothing but darkness and intent looking into Stephan's eyes. It was accompanied with desperation and determination of a man who felt betrayed, and this was a dangerous combination.

"Oh, jeez." The doctor mumbled under his breath.

"Look through his desk, Stephan. I think you will be delighted with what you find." The demon whispered. It was sitting on top of the lie detector machine and swinging its long legs gleefully like a young child. Stephan took his seat in the doctor's chair behind the large, heavy desk.

"All right, Krochek. You seem a bit anxious right now. Do I make you anxious?" He asked as he pointed the scalpel at the doctor. He opened desk drawers. In the top left drawer he found a picture frame. The doctor had his arms around a woman and two children. "Well, well, well. What's this?"

"That's nothing." Dr. Krochek waved his hand and acted aloof.

"It has to be something if you keep it in your top desk drawer, my friend. I'm guessing . . . wife and kids. Damn, your wife has a nice set on her. Bet you have some fun squeezing those, huh, doc?" Stephan made a squeezing motion with his hand that had the scalpel in it. "How the hell does a guy like you get to be so lucky, when you don't even come close to deserving it?" Stephan asked, squinting at the doctor.

"What are you doing?" The doctor asked him as he shook his head and looked away. Dr. Krochek had a horrible feeling in his stomach, and it made him nauseous. He tried to keep hot tears from forming in his eyes from the horrid feeling he had that started gnawing at him in his subconscious.

"What am I doing?" Stephan laughed. "What am I doing? What's going on? What did you just give me? What meds did you put me on? Take your pick of any question like this, and that is the question of the day. The answer to you is the same that was always given to me. Fuck you! Didn't I want the answer to that same question . . . and what bull shit did you give me? Lies, lies and more lies!" Stephan pulled the long wires from the lie detector machine. "I'm not going to kill you . . . but I think what I am going to is, make you wish you were dead." He made his way to where the doctor was sitting, and bound him tightly to the chair using the wires. He continued to rifle throughout the office. He found the tablets of every patient currently admitted to the hospital in a filing cabinet behind the desk. He found his and started to look for Rosie's. Dr. Krochek allowed a few minutes to pass before he finally spoke.

"You're looking for Rosalie Carmichael, aren't you?" He said, breaking Stephan's concentration.

"Yeah, what about it." He replied, still searching through tablets.

"You won't find her."

"What the fuck do you mean?" Stephan paused and glared at Dr. Krochek.

"She died."

"BULL SHIT! It's just another lie! I can't believe any of the trash coming out of your decrepit mouth! I should cut out your damn tongue to save anyone from hearing your lies ever again!" Stephan twisted the scalpel at him.

"Why lie to you now when you have the upper hand?" Dr. Krochek asked him. Stephan frantically looked for Rosalie's tablet, but after what seemed like hours of searching, it wasn't there. Tablets littered the floor, but none of them were Rosie's. Stephan pulled his tablet from his pocket and threw it into the pile with all the others.

"Then none of it will matter . . ." His voice trailed off for a moment. "How did it happen?" He asked quietly.

"She had a negative reaction to medication."

"I'm supposed to believe that. You were giving her the drugs that killed her." Stephan suddenly growled at him. He picked up the picture of the doctor's family again, and tapped the glass with the point of the scalpel. "I bet if I looked hard enough, I could find your address somewhere in this office." Stephan got a sickening smile on his face. He dropped the photo and cracked the glass of the frame. He played with the scalpel with his fingertips, and lowered his eyes at the doctor. "Let's play . . . find the shrinks' wallet!" He opened the thin drawer in front of the desk, and shook his head as he looked at the doctor. "Not in there. Now . . . a wallet is more of a thing that you would keep in a back pocket, you would think." Stephan sauntered over to Dr. Krochek. The doctor had already adjusted himself in the chair to prevent Stephan from retrieving what was in his back pocket. "You're forgetting who is in charge here, doc. Now I think you should play nice." Stephan grabbed the doctor by the back of his hair and yanked his head backwards violently. He held the scalpel blade a mere millimeter away from the doctor's eye. "You wouldn't want to go missing anything else now, would you?" At this threat, he allowed access to his back pocket where he kept his black, leather wallet, and Stephan pulled back the blade. "What a bitch, you wouldn't give your eye for your family. I'll be sure to let your wife know that before I . . . well . . . you know exactly . . . what I'm capable of, don't you?" Stephan walked back over to the chair behind the desk and sat down. He propped his feet upon the desk and opened the wallet. "Look at this . . . more pictures of the same people. I must say doc . . . I never expected someone like you to do so well in the wifey department. My God, what does she see in you? You must be making bank." He pulled out the doctor's drivers license. "Victor Igor Krochek? Good God . . . Did your parents hate you? Nice mug shot. Oh, I hate to tell you . . . I know this neighborhood. The ex and I didn't live too far from there. I think we actually looked at a house on Beechwood Terrace if my memory serves me correctly, but my memory isn't so good because of those drugs you had me on." Stephan gave a small smile at the memory, and at the fact he could make the doctor uncomfortable.

"Beechwood is nice. Some beautiful houses." Dr. Krochek mumbled.

"Oh please, tell me you're not trying to be friends with me now, because it's a little late for that." Stephan put the doctor's license in his pocket. "Now I know you have a key card. What am I going to have to cut out or off of you to get that from you?"

"Nothing, I'll give you the card . . . just if you get out of here, don't hurt my family . . . please! They did nothing to you! Take your freedom and be happy with it! I'll destroy your records! It will be as if you were never here! Just don't hurt my family, please! Please!" Dr. Krochek begged tearfully. "The key card is in the back of the top drawer . . . under the organization tray."

"You're absolutely right. They didn't do a damn thing to me." Stephan wrote the number to Dr. Krochek's desk phone down on the back of his hand with a pen, "but you did." He patted the doctor on the shoulder. "The next time we meet, it'll be in hell, doc." Those were the last words he spoke to the doctor before he left the office. He made his way down the corridor to the second set of double doors that would lead him back to the unit. He used the doctor's card, and it worked like a charm. He went through the doors quietly. The hallway was dimly lit as well to conserve energy for the generator. The unit appeared to be a ghost town. He eyed his old room. He opened the door far enough for it to stay open.

He went to the mattress, hoping the piece of metal Rosie gave him was still there. Luckily, it was, and he slid it in the strike plate like he had done before. He allowed the door to close, and he waited in the dark as he looked through the window. He knew someone was working, and he didn't want to take the chance of running into an orderly or a nurse. He would probably have to kill them, and he wasn't sure how far the scalpel was going to take him.

Stephan waited for almost ten minutes before he started formulating another plan until he saw her . . . Nurse Adams. He could barely contain his excitement. He saw her hand fidgeting with the antenna of the battery powered radio. He pounded hard on the door with his fist, and peeked through the window. It took a second, but he saw Nurse Adams' head poke around the corner of the nurses station and look down the hall. When she went back behind the desk, he pounded again. This time she stepped out from the desk, and put her hands on her hips. She had an annoyed look on her face, but at the same time, he could tell she was expecting it to happen again. Stephan decided to hold her in suspense. Just as she was about to turn back to the nurse's station, he pounded again. This time she quickly twisted around and glared down the hall, but she had a bit of fear in her eye. She wondered where the sound came from. A likely scenario was a patient was out of bed, and was being disruptive because of the storm. Stephan ducked off to the side when she grabbed a flashlight from the desk, and began to check the sleeping patients. She passed over Stephan's room, because she assumed it was empty. No one had been in that room since he proceeded to a control room. He waited for her to be at the end of the hall checking patients to peek through the window, and pounded again. Nurse Adams was trying not to get fearful, but right now she was alone, and what was happening was strange. She just saw all the patients were asleep. She approached Stephan's old room, and cracked the door open. Stephan stepped back into the shadowy corner. The bed was neatly made, ready for the next intake. She opened the door a bit more and stepped inside.

"You're being stupid Tracy." She said out loud to herself. She stood in the middle of the room, and let out a long sigh. It took her a moment to realize the room was gradually getting darker. Stephan was slowly closing the door on both of them.

"You're being stupid Tracy. Acceptance *is* the first step." Nurse Adams jumped out of her skin, and uttered a short, shrill cry. She didn't know whom she was looking at until she shakily raised the flashlight and saw Stephan's face. "Stephan! How did you get out of the control room?" Her tone changed from fearful to unsparing, yet inquisitive.

"Oh, if only you knew what else I've been up to . . . you would have a much different question to ask me."

"What else have you been up too?" Nurse Adams asked quietly. Stephan didn't say anything, instead he gave her an impish smile. A sudden wave of uneasiness took over Nurse Adams. Her stomach knotted up from a tension brought on by the sudden fear. The nurse's intuition told her something horrible was about to happen.

"Well, I had to pay a little visit to Krochek on my way here from the control room. You and I both know that was totally unavoidable."

"Victor. What did you do to Vic . . . .?" She said shakily.

"He had to learn a lesson. Just like you." "Oh no, you . . . killed him?" She asked.

"I don't think you have the right to want any information out of me, considering how you were with me. You bitch. I believe I wanted information from you and I got strapped to a bed for it."

"Please just tell me."

"I'll tell you what I want to tell you." He paused and looked at the nurse in the dim light. "This is the second time I had a woman in this room. The first one . . . much sexier, and we had a lot of fun. Do you think we could have fun . . . Tracy?

"Just tell me what you did to Vic." She demanded Stephan.

"Oh my God! You never stop barking orders! Seriously, you're in love with him, or you have been fucking him. Which is it?" He laughed heartily at the thought of the couple.

"Well, you think that's so funny . . . It's written up that Rosalie Carmichael died of a bad reaction to meds . . . but the truth is . . . I killed her. I found out she was pregnant." Nurse Adams slowly walked towards the door. Through the window, she could see the young orderly and nurse arguing with one another in the hallway. "I don't know how you two managed to do it, but you knocked her up, and she was pregnant with your little bastard." She continued to rock on her feet slowly towards the door. "The hospital didn't need that kind of heat. Victor didn't need that kind publicity. I did what I had to do."

"Rosie was pregnant. What exactly did you do?" Stephan asked as tears fell from his unblinking eyes. His jaw was clenched as he listened intently.

"I gave her a morphine overdose, and she was cremated before an official autopsy could be done. We had a Coroner who does favors for us sign her death certificate. She was four months along." Nurse Adams was getting enjoyment from telling him this, even though there was a part of her that was very much afraid of Stephan at this moment. She was alone in the dark room with a psychopath during a storm. She had seen this movie before.

"Make her pay, Stephan. You know she deserves it. She took your child, and the love of your life had to pay. Make her suffer." The demon appeared by the window. Its eyes burned and lit the room up like a dark room again.

"All because you didn't want her having my baby? You could have just let us go. It never would have come to this."

"Come to what." Nurse Adams saw the glint of the metal scalpel in Stephan's hand for the first time. "Stephan, now is not the time to do anything you're going to regret." She was still out of reach of the door to pound on it to gain the attention of the nurse and orderly outside.

"I could never regret this." He grabbed Nurse Adams by the front of her blouse. She dug her nails into his arm deep enough to draw blood, but it didn't loosen his grip at all. "This has been a long time coming." He sank the scalpel into her side rapidly and repeatedly, and let her crumple to the floor. It happened quickly, and Stephan was in a dizzy haze throughout the duration of his crime. Nurse Adams didn't have a chance to scream, only gasp as he literally swept her off of her feet. He finally gathered clarity, and heard the blood drip from his hand and the scalpel, and hit the tile floor. He felt himself shaking from the adrenaline. Stephan bent over her and listened, "hmm, you're still breathing . . . now that's a problem. Bitches aren't allowed to breathe." He grabbed a hold of the top of her hair, and put her in a seated position. He crouched behind her, and found the silver chain that held the dreaded whistle she used to blow to have her hounds take him down. He pulled it as tightly as he could against her trachea. Nurse Adams gagged and gasped, and her hands clawed at the air in front of her. She desperately tried to grab hold of Stephan behind her to stop him, but he stayed out of reach. He was too much for her and she was overpowered. Her fighting began to lessen, until it ceased. When he felt that she finally had succumb to her injuries, he released his grip on the chain. He allowed her to slump to the floor with an ugly thud. "I believe the Lord's work has been done here today." Stephan said as he stood up. The red glow lessened and was part of the shadow again. He stared at the intense red orbs engulfed in the shadow. He could feel the satisfaction the demon had gotten from what he had done. He cleaned the blood off of the scalpel with the nurse's uniform and went to the door. He carefully peered through the window and no one was in sight. The nurse and orderly finished their argument and moved along to other things. Thankfully, they evaded Stephan's rampage.

Stephan looked at the shadow angrily.

"You were supposed to get Rosie out too."

"She did get out, you didn't specify how she would get out." The demon smiled at Stephan.

"You said she would be okay." He said, glaring at the red orbs.

"Who's to say she isn't all right where she is?" The shadow laughed. Stephan grunted with anger. He took a second look out of the window. He opened the door and removed the rectangular plate. He closed the door quietly behind him. He didn't want the body being discovered quite yet. At least now he knew no one would be going to Dr. Krochek's office while he was tied up. Stephan was still armed with the scalpel, and still carried the doctor's drivers license as he made his way to the cafeteria. He went behind the buffet bar, and through a doorway that led into the kitchen. He saw the door along the wall that led to the basement next to an elevator. That was really his only option right now, he couldn't just walk out the front door. Stephan made his way down the rickety, wooden steps, and found himself in a large basement with smooth, concrete floors. He followed the noise of the generator, and looked inside a small room. He saw feet wearing worn, steel toe boots poking out from the end of a bed. Stephan put it all together. This was the driver of the truck that he watched from his window. He saw the door with snow blowing in underneath. He went over to it and cracked it open. Outside, he saw the faded, green truck parked and waiting for him to take it. He could have an escape vehicle if he played his cards right. He peeked into the room again and noticed the man had fallen asleep while reading a book. He quietly snuck into the room and held the scalpel to the man's throat. He shook him slightly to rouse him from his slumber.

"Give me the keys to the truck and I won't slit you open." Stephan ordered. The shocked and scared man just pointed wide eyed, with a quivering finger to a small set of keys on top of a makeshift bookshelf in the corner. "Got any clothes besides these gowns?" Pete said nothing, but shifted his pointing finger to a dresser. Stephan found a pair of black pants that went with a blue sweater to wear. He was also lucky enough to find a pair of shoes that were only a half size too large. "Thank you." Being true to his word, Stephan did not cut Pete's throat. He got into the truck, and started it. The adrenaline was pumping like PCP through his veins. He had made it this far, and no one was going to stop him now.

CHAPTER 15

Rosie was dead. One of the reasons he was doing this, was gone. She was murdered by someone who was his adversary, until he had gotten justice for her. But still, he was left to suffer a broken heart. This time it felt much differently. It felt like a piece of himself was missing. It didn't feel that way with Sandy when she decided to leave him. Losing Rosie was making him feel like his heart was dying slowly, and soon, there would be nothing but a hardened, black rock. He didn't want to live anymore. He finally understood Paul and how he wanted to die. No matter the reason he had, Stephan finally understood it. He knew he was eventually going to go down for what he planned to do, but Stephan didn't care anymore. He had nothing left to care for, and he figured he might as well give in to his darkness, and let it guide him. If he was going to go down, he wasn't going to go down alone. He was going to take as many with him as he could, and he had already started back at the hospital.

Orroth, the demon sat in the passenger seat of the truck as Stephan drove. His eyes glowed brilliantly, and his smile was wide with excitement. It had waited for so long for Stephan to hear it, and now he was doing everything it wanted.

"What you have planned for the doctor is going to devastate him." Orroth's voice was hoarse and almost monotone, but the joy could still be heard in its depths.

"That's the point. An eye for an eye, but I'm collecting with interest. I thought *you* of all things would understand that." Stephan murmured.

"Oh, no judgments. I happen to think what you're about to do is . . . delightful." The demon's voice lowered to a harsh whisper. "I can't wait to see the beautiful demise you will create. What happened with the woman . . . was . . . unavoidable." Stephan's eyes narrowed, and a vindictive grin spread across his face.

"He's going to pay for what he's done in the exact same way I had to pay." He began to think about whether he should go to Dr. Krochek's house or his ex-wife's first. Either way, they were both being paid a visit tonight. He rested on the decision to see the doctor's family first. *Just in case that bastard manages to untie himself somehow, let's see what his family is up to during this stormy night.'* Stephan thought to himself. He looked at the time on the digital clock the truck console . . . 10:44 P.M. They were more than likely in bed. He drove passed and saw the house was dark, but it was hard to tell because most of the neighborhoods had lost power. He parked the truck at a convenience store a quarter mile down the road, and walked to the Krochek residence under the cover of night. He made his way to the back door, and waited for a gust of wind to howl to break the window. He reached through and unlocked the door. He stealthily made his way inside and took a moment to take in his surroundings.

'Gotta give Krochek props! He is a man of wealth and taste!' Stephan thought as he looked around. The kitchen had marble counter tops and the latest appliances. When he looked in the living room, the size of the television was unnecessarily large. The custom stone used to make the enormous fireplace was as arrogant as the doctor and looked as if it cost quite a large sum of money to have it finished for him. The furniture looked comfortable, yet expensive. In a room on the other side of the living room was a dining room that was also attached to the kitchen. He could see a large, rectangular table surrounded by chairs inside of the room. Stephan became white hot with anger as he imagined the doctor having joyous dinner parties while patients wasted away in the hospital, and paid for his caviar and champagne. Stephan sighed in disgust, knowing what the

doctor did to get everything. He finally made his ascent upstairs. Along the way he observed photos of family vacations and Christmas'. Photographs of their growing children littered the wall. Stephan was seeing Dr. Krochek as the normal family man, and not as the dry psychiatrist. He continued to creep up the stairs being careful not to make a sound. His breathing was shallow, and every step was with purpose. He stepped in front of the first bedroom door, and slowly and silently opened it. He began to hear his own thudding heartbeat in his ears. It was Dr. Krochek's seventeen year old daughter's room, and she was fast asleep in her canopy bed. For a moment Stephan questioned himself, and if he could follow through with his plan when he saw her Harvard acceptance letter on her night stand. His hands began to shake, and the thumping in his ears grew louder into a swishing sound that spread into his head when he remembered what the doctor took from him. His eyes suddenly changed into tunnel vision. Without thinking twice, he set his hand gently on her head to keep it still. In one fluid motion, he sank the scalpel into the girl's carotid artery and severed it. She didn't move or wake up. It was quick and painless for her. Stephan was still looking through a black tunnel, but the swishing had suddenly silenced itself. He could only hear his quivering, shallow breathing. He stood in the hallway and looked at the blood on his hands. His stomach began to churn, but a thought that wasn't his own, intruded his mind. It was the voice of Orroth, *'you can't turn back now, keep going!'* Stephan found his senses again, and made his way to the second bedroom door across the hall, where there was a sixteen-year-old boy snoring softly in an entanglement of blankets. He knew it was too late to turn back now, the demon even said it was. He had already killed the girl and Nurse Adams. Without thinking, he sank the scalpel into Dr. Krochek's son's artery just as he had the daughter. He slept through it just as his sister had, which relieved Stephan. Killing the children was the hardest part for him, but he felt it had to be done to vindicate Rosie and the part of his life that was stolen from him. He crept back the hallway further and found a wireless phone sitting on a small table next to a bouquet of silk flowers. Stephan picked it up and saw that it lit up. *'Krochek must have a generator.'* Stephan thought. He took the phone and quietly made his way back downstairs. He made himself comfortable in a cozy looking recliner. He dialed the number he wrote down on his hand from the desk phone in Dr Krochek's office. It rang four times on the other line before the voice mail finally picked up.

"You have reached the desk of Dr. Victor Krochek. I am away from my desk. Please leave a brief message with your name and number, and I will return your call as soon as possible." An automated voice took over, and told Stephan to record a message after the tone. He was finally able to record what he wanted to say to Dr. Krochek.

"Hey doc, I'm calling from inside your home." He said in a low tone. "I must say that you have impeccable taste. I do have some bad news for you though, and it's that the scalpel I had . . . found its way into your kids, and I don't think they're gonna make it. Now, I do kinda feel bad about that. More bad news . . . I'm about to go where your wife is sleeping, and do the same to her. I'm going to call you back, so you can hear her die. Bye bye for now." Stephan hung up the phone and stood up. He looked at the scalpel in his blood-covered hand, and decided to get a better tool. He made his way into the kitchen and dropped the scalpel in the trash compactor. He began rummaging through the drawers for a sharp knife. Most of what he found was dull, and he was unsatisfied with his findings. He went into the dining room and searched through an oak china cabinet. He found a long, black box with lovely, silver clasps. He gently opened it to find a beautiful carving knife, nestled in red velvet. Along the top of the lid, in silver cursive were the letters, *'Congratulations.'* He took a moment to admire the craftsmanship of the blade. Stephan assumed it was only used on special occasions, and this was a very special occasion, especially for Stephan. He started his ascension upstairs again until he noticed a small light through a cracked open door. There was a room set off from the living room. Stephan didn't notice it before, because he was too preoccupied drinking in the doctor's material possessions and making the voice mail to Dr. Krochek. He stopped, and curiosity got the better of him. He opened the door a bit more and poked his head inside. *'Krochek's home office.'* He debated on going through the room and putting off what he had to do upstairs. He decided to take care of the wife first, and then he would see what the room had to offer. He slowly made his way upstairs, yet again. He crept back to the end of the hallway. He stopped at the door and grasped the ornate handle. He slowly and quietly opened the door. The small amount of light that came through the bedroom window allowed him to observe the lump under the blankets that was Dr. Krochek's wife. Stephan's steps were deliberate as he approached the sleeping woman. Eventually, he was right next to the bed looking down upon her. He held his new knife with a firm grip in one hand, and reached out and touched her shoulder with his other to stir her. At first, all she did was let out a small moan until Stephan touched her again, and she turned and looked up at the person who was waking her. Mrs. Krochek was expecting to see her husband or one of her children, not an escaped mental patient with a large knife. She opened her mouth to scream, but Stephan stopped her by putting his free hand over her mouth. He left a slight red smear of blood on her face that was left on his hands that hadn't dried yet.

"Now . . . don't go doing that. That's just going to piss me off more, and this is going to end a whole lot worse for you." He said calmly and quietly. Instead of screaming, she began to sob and hyperventilate. He removed his hand from her mouth. Stephan turned on the bedside lamp, and Mrs. Krochek let out a panicked cry when she saw her carving knife in Stephan's possession along with the blood on his hand. He looked at her, and then at the knife. "You're afraid of what my plans are . . ." He sighed. "Let's just get right to why I'm here. Do you know what your husband does?" Stephan asked as he sat down next to her, the knife still in hand. She inched away from him and grabbed a hold of the bed's headboard.

"He helps . . . the mentally . . . ill. He's a . . . good . . . man." She managed to stumble out between sobs. "Whose blood . . . is . . . that?"

"Wow, so he even has you fooled." Stephan mumbled. He let out a long sigh, "it's not important where this blood came from." Stephan turned his bloody hand around and analyzed it. "I'm here to explain something important to you. I hate to be the one to break it to you, but your good man of a husband . . . is actually a monster. The mentally ill you think he's helping never leave that hospital again. Every last one . . . an experiment . . . just another number that pays for your vacations and delightful dinner parties. Your husband had someone killed to save his experiment. Whom he killed meant something to me. Maybe now you can understand why this is happening to you."

"What's happening . . . what else . . . is going to happen to me? Who are you? How . . . do you know . . . my husband?" She asked shakily.

"I was one of his patients, deary." Stephan gave her small sideways smile. Orroth emerged in the corner with a powerful groan.

"It's time to deal with her. Time is running out." The demon ordered. Stephan obediently dialed the doctor's desk phone.

"By the way, this wouldn't be happening to you if your husband wasn't such a coward and gave me his eye in exchange for his wallet. He was quick to give up that wallet when I had a scalpel to his cornea though." Stephan told Mrs. Krochek, while he waited to leave a message. "Guess who, doc! Someone here wants to say hello." Stephan held the phone up Mrs. Krochek. "Speak like it's the last time you're ever going to talk to him." Stephan advised her ominously. She looked at him with watery, fearful brown eyes.

"I . . . love you . . . Vic. If anything . . . happens . . . to me. Take . . . care . . . ", she paused and swallowed, because she wouldn't be able to get the next words out if she didn't, "take care . . . of . . . the kids. Tell them . . . every day . . . I love them. I love you . . . my husband." With one quick motion, Stephan slashed the silver knife across Mrs. Krochek's throat. He continued to hold the phone close to her. As he had promised, Dr. Krochek would hear his wife's dying breath. She gargled and choked on the blood that pooled in the back of her throat and she fell backwards. The blood slowly drowned her, and Stephan got every moment for the doctor to hear. He hung up the phone, and threw it next to the doctor's wife's body and turned off the light. He exited the room, taking the knife with him. He briskly made his way for the doctor's home office downstairs.

The first thing he wanted to go through was the desk. He sat behind it and thoroughly searched through it, but found nothing that would be of any use to him. He eyed the built in bookshelves along the wall. He sat back in the desk chair and rubbed his chin in deep thought. He knew about hidden wall safes and Dr. Krochek seemed like the type of man to have one, considering the rest of his home. He stood up and started pulling books from the shelves. He began to throw them to the floor until he reached one that didn't pull from the shelf, but only tilted slightly. A section of bookshelf lifted slightly, and popped open with a loud click. It had now become a doorway leading somewhere the doctor had kept hidden. Stephan was in for more than he had bargained for. He was expecting a hidden safe, but instead he found a hidden passageway to the unknown.

Stephan pushed the pile of books he tore from the shelves, aside from the hidden doorway. The door opened more, and he saw there was a set of stairs leading down into a hidden basement. A light was on at the bottom, but Stephan was still careful to approach the hidden room. At the bottom of the stairs, there was nothing more than a small, unremarkable area. Dr. Krochek had it set up as a hidden office. His wife probably didn't know about her husband's secret place. There was a desk in the center of the room with an old chair. A small lamp on the desk was the source of light that Stephan was seeing earlier. There was a small stack of manila folders on top of the desk. He sat down, and began to read their contents. After he had gotten so far into what he was reading, his jaw dropped when he realized what he had in his hands. These were the secrets that Dr. Krochek, Dr. Montgomery, Dr. Wagner and Nurse Adam's worked so hard to cover up. Rosie wasn't the only patient that had died under the care of the hospital. The documents consisted of reports of patient neglect and deaths that Dr. Krochek and the others kept quiet. Complaints of employee misconduct that was covered up to keep the hospital open. Stephan turned his attention to the desk drawers. In the top drawer, he found a Beretta M9 Luger semi automatic with a box of ammunition. "Well, that's an upgrade. What's a doctor need a gun like that for?" Stephan said out loud. He was very pleased with his discoveries so far, despite his questions. He also found a bottle of Jameson whiskey that only had a couple shots taken out of it. For the moment, Stephan felt like a lucky man again. The feeling was diminished to anger when he thought about not having Rosie to share it with, and he knew he had to keep going. He had to plan his next moves out very carefully. He took everything he had found, and decided at this time that taking the truck would be too risky because the police could be looking for him to be driving it by now. His paranoia was setting in at full tilt now that he had killed four people. He looked in the garage, and saw a black SUV parked in one of the stalls. He looked around for keys, and eventually found them in Mrs. Krochek's purse by her bed. He quickly made his way back to the garage, and hoisted himself into the vehicle and started it. The garage door automatically opened and Stephan's heart skipped a beat. He wasn't used to the high end technology that the higher class could afford, like garage doors that automatically opened when you started your car.

"Hello Mrs. Krochek. What is your destination?" A robotic female voice asked. Stephan let out a sigh of relief, turned on manual drive, and backed out of the garage. He drove passed the convenience store where he left the truck, and glanced at it quickly. It sat there, abandoned. No police were surrounding it, and there was no yellow tape. He began the drive to his ex-wife's house. He couldn't wait to see whom she had in bed with her, because he was going to kill him too. When he got close to Sandy's house, Stephan pulled the SUV up a back road that ran beside her house. He turned the lights off, and parked the SUV. A thick row of trees hid the dark vehicle from sight. He gathered the folders, gun, ammunition and whiskey, and started the walk to her house. He entered through the back door.

He knew she would have it unlocked, because she always forgot to lock that door. Stephan always remembered for them when he lived there. He used to keep her safe from danger, but now he was the danger.

CHAPTER 16

No one was awake in Sandy's house. Stephan peered into the living room. His ex-wife had rearranged the furniture since he had last been in the house. It all seemed so familiar, and yet strange at the same time. It was as if he was there in his body, but looking at everything through someone's eyes that were seeing it for the first time. It was the same furniture and appliances, but he was a stranger there now. He was unwelcome. He saw that Sandy kept his favorite chair. He flopped down in it, and placed the gun on the table next to him with the manila folders underneath it. He opened the bottle of whiskey and took a swig from it. Stephan was content sitting and drinking for a moment while holding the box of ammunition. He began to look around at the pictures that were displayed. When he realized what they were pictures of, he wanted to lose what he had just drank. In the photographs, was Mr. S in a ball cap. He had his arms around Sandy from behind. In another photo, he was kissing her cheek as she smiled brightly. She looked happier with Mr. S then she ever had been with him. Stephan sank back in the chair. He held the bottle of whiskey on his knee, and let out a shaky sigh.

"Here's to being fucking right." He whispered with a rising, burning rage as he raised the bottle in the air. He sucked at the bottle, and fought the urge to regurgitate. He set the bottle on the table and quickly became slightly inebriated from the alcohol. Stephan was seething from what he saw and everything else he had found out throughout the night. He grabbed the gun, loaded it, and tossed the rest of the ammunition on the small table. He put the gun in the back of his pants, and grasped the manila folders in the hand that was starting to shed small particles of dried blood. He looked up the stairs, and smiled darkly. He knew what he was about to do. Adrenaline kicked in, and began to take over his alcoholic stupor. It gave him a feeling of energized sobriety. Time slowed down for Stephan as he approached Sandy's bedroom door. It was as if he reached for the door knob and opened the door in slow motion. Everything was silent for the moments that he observed Sandy sleeping next to her new significant other. He could faintly see Mr. S' glasses on the night stand. It was the same night stand that used to be Stephan's. It was the same bed and dresser. It seemed as though, the only thing's Sandy wanted replaced were the sheets and man she slept with. She moved this man in to replace Stephan like he was the mistake that had to be gotten rid of quickly. She wanted the same life, but a different partner. What safer replacement than the therapist treating that said mistake? Stephan hit the light switch, but neither of them was roused.

"Wake up! Wake the fuck up liars, cheats and whores!" Sandy shot straight up. Sleep left her eyes immediately, and was replaced by a look of shock when she saw it was her ex-husband. Mr. S fumbled with his glasses and finally got him on his face, but was still half-lid from sleep. He finally managed to see that it was Stephan standing in his bedroom. "Now that I have your attention. Today is a special day for all the liars, traitors and adulterers."

"Stephan! What the FUCK are you doing in here? How did you get out of the hospital?" Sandy demanded, with all the authority she could muster in her position.

"Oh, didn't the wormy little fuck face tell ya? They let me out on account of my fabulous recovery and good behavior." Stephan stated, with a cheeky smile.

"What . . . that's not true . . . when . . ." Mr. S mumbled while trying to shake the sleep from his head.

"Don't bother arguing with him, John. He's being sarcastic." Sandy said with disgust. "There is absolutely no way Dr. Krochek would've let you out."

"Wait! Your name is John Stevens? What a white bread name. Fuck dude . . . you're a dick's inch away from being a John Smith!" Stephan laughed." This is what you wanted instead of me? Seriously?" He asked Sandy rhetorically.

"You're a complete fuck wad." Mr. S said, finally realizing the situation.

"What is that exactly? A wad of fucks . . . now, I called you a wormy . . . fuck face . . . that has meaning. You wormed your way into my life. Completely sabotaged me, and as far as the fuck face . . . well, you have a face, and I do wanna fuck . . . it . . . up." Stephan admitted with a smile.

"I don't have to put up with this in my own home!" Mr. S started to get out of bed.

"Nuh-uh, there lover boy." Stephan pulled the gun out of the back of his pants and waved it at him. All the blood drained away from Mr. S' face, and he slowly sat back down on the bed. "Your house, huh? Did you buy it after going through all the real estate agents? Did you build a business with your own blood, sweat and tears, and make a name for yourself? Did you earn what all this has become? I am the one that gave this life to this ungrateful bitch!" Stephan shouted as he pointed to Sandy. "I gotta know . . . how long was it going on behind my back . . . you know . . . before I went in the hospital?" Stephan asked Sandy.

"It's not what you think. You're going to think this happened to you to sabotage you . . ." Sandy said.

"Just answer the damn question." Stephan asked again quietly, cutting her off.

"You're going to take it the wrong way. Like it was all against you . . . but it wasn't like that at all."

"Why are trying so hard to defend yourself if it was nothing? Why won't you just answer the damn question?"

"Stephan, just put the gun down. Please." Sandy whispered.

"Bitch! What makes you think I have to do anything you say? You wanted the divorce which gave me my balls back! I will make you eat this gun if I want to, you Judas! Now, how long?" Stephan screamed. He was getting impatient. He made his way over to Sandy, and got the gun ready to fire. She looked into his eyes, and saw a hatred she had never seen before. At that moment, Sandy was ultimately afraid of her ex-husband. She didn't know what he was planning to do if she didn't cooperate. She knew she had better give him the answer he desired, because he already knew the truth deep down inside.

"I started seeing him a month before your hospitalization." Sandy finally said. Mr. S sighed in disbelief, and mumbled to himself. She was going to tell him the truth, and get them both killed.

"Now I'm really interested in what your definition of 'seeing' is? That could mean lots of things. I saw my secretary at work, but it was innocent. God loves that silver haired prude, she got the job done."

"I started seeing him for his professional services. It didn't start out sexual, but after seeing him a few times for legitimate therapy, it evolved into that. He was listening when you weren't. You completely checked out of reality, and our marriage."

"Did you even try to talk to me? No . . . you didn't. You just pulled some name out of a hat, decided to fuck him, and . . . screw up my whole entire life in the process!"

"It's not like we sought out to sabotage you." Sandy mumbled. Stephan turned and sat in a chair in the corner of the room.

"I gotta say . . . it looks different from this angle." Stephan stared at the floor. He didn't notice Mr. S grab his cell phone and send an emergency text to 9-1-1, telling them that they had a dangerous intruder in their home holding them hostage at gunpoint. "Where did I go wrong? What did I do that was so wrong Sandy? I just want to know, I'm curious."

"You were acting crazy most of the time. Sometimes talking to things that weren't there. You were always so bitter and sarcastic. You were so hard to get along with sometimes. Always drinking and getting high. I could barely get a sober word out of you. I wanted to move on with life . . . and have a family, and having a baby with you . . . I just couldn't see it."

"Okay, if it was that bad. Why not just divorce me? Why was I not allowed to have a life of my own without you? Why couldn't I have a happy ending too?" Sandy was silent, and played nervously with the hem of the lilac colored top sheet. Stephan thought for a moment, and a sideways grin spread across his face. "You wanted it all to yourself. The house, business, savings accounts. You . . . selfish bitch." Sandy still couldn't make eye contact with him. "I can always tell when you're guilty. You can't look me in the eye." He managed a laugh. "Well! Look at the nasty mess you made! If you think about it . . . all this could have been avoided if you weren't so damn selfish and treacherous. This would be the definition of ultimate betrayal. I thought I knew you, but you have proven me wrong. I knew nothing about you! Who really is this stranger here?" Stephan stood up and peeked through the curtain. His paranoia was acting up again. He closed the curtain, and stood at the end of the bed.

"No matter how you spin it, you have a diagnosis. You need to be in the hospital." Mr. S said.

"Oh, after what I did tonight, they won't be sending me to any hospitals." Stephan let out a chuckle.

"What did you do?" Sandy whispered. Stephan debated on whether or not he should tell them what he did. He turned and gave her the most sadistic smile he could. His eyes became darkened, and almost hollowed as he lowered them to hers. He raised his bloody hand. It was beginning to darken and crack, but you could still tell it was blood.

"I killed Krochek's wife and kids. To make it better . . . I called his office phone, and there is a voice mail recording of his wife's last breath." He said coldly, but maintaining the savage smile upon his face. "That son of a cock sucker will love hearing the love of his life, slowly gagging and drowning on her own blood."

"Oh shit . . ." Mr. S threw up on the floor next to bed as soon as he heard Stephan say that.

"Some man you got there." Stephan snickered. "I bet he cries when rainbows come out to play." Just as Stephan said that. A faint reflection of red and blue flashes bounced off of the tan walls of the bedroom. He laughed out loud, and moved the curtain aside. Six police cars were parked outside. The men had their guns drawn, and they were preparing to deal with a hostage situation. "How the fuck did they know to come here?" He murmured inquisitively.

"9-1-1 text asshole!" Mr. S blurted out, with a satisfied smile. He reveled in the moment that he had outsmarted Stephan, and rescued himself and Sandy. He would be a hero, and would get his fifteen minutes of fame. He would be on the news as the man who took down the notorious, escaped mental patient.

Unfortunately, his plans were to be foiled. Stephan saw things ending differently. He paced back over to the end of the bed.

"Well, I guess that means we will be wrapping things up sooner than expected." Stephan said coolly. "Sandy, do you love John?"

"Yes." She replied arrogantly. "That's a stupid question." She didn't hesitate when she answered.

"That's good, that's really good." Stephan suddenly aimed the pistol at Mr. S, and squeezed the trigger. The bullet went through the lens of his glasses, and into his left eye. He instantly collapsed against Sandy which made her release a bloodcurdling scream. "YOU SAID YOU LOVED HIM! WHAT'S THE MATTER WITH HIM NOW? YOU DON'T LOVE HIM ANYMORE? ISN'T HE GOOD ENOUGH FOR THE PRINCESS NOW?" Stephan screamed at her.

She started shaking her head in disbelief, and mumbling incoherently while she sobbed. Stephan assumed it was her begging for him not to end her life as well. "They say the eyes are the windows to the soul. I didn't see anything leave him. I wonder if that means he had no soul. Someone who could split up a marriage . . . has to be without a soul." Stephan rambled as he readied the gun to fire again. "I should be thanking you for sending me to the hospital, really. It made me realize how much I hate you, and how shitty a person you truly are. I also met my real true love there, even though she's gone now. A man like me never deserved someone like her anyway. She was far too perfect, and I wouldn't have wanted to destroy someone so divine. Alas, the doctor and his bitch lackey destroyed such a beautiful creature. I had the privilege to make the sweetest love to her for a whole night. It was better than I ever had with you or anyone ever." Stephan smiled as he remembered the night Rosie had snuck into his room. Sandy continued to sob and was frozen to the blood spattered bed. She quietly implored him to let her live.

"You can have the house back, and your business, Stephan." He smiled, shook his head and finally let out a laugh. He ignored all her pleading and negotiating as he raised the gun to her, and squeezed. Yet again, time slowed down for Stephan. The bullet seemed to take longer to hit Sandy than it did Mr. S, but when it finally made contact, it pierced through her heart. It killed her almost instantly.

"Well, well, would you look at that . . . you had a heart after all." Stephan joked. He wasted no time grabbing the manila folders. It was his time to shine. He knew it was going to come to this one way or another. He finished what he had to do, and at least he would be at peace knowing that. The contents of the manila folders needed to get to the police now. That was the best place for it all right now, especially after everything that had happened that night. Stephan escaped from an institution, and killed six people within mere hours. What was about to happen, was well deserved for the man who committed such crimes.

Orroth smiled at him from the corner of the bedroom. Its eyes still burning red like hot fire. Stephan stood still and waited for it to speak. "Look at what you've done, Stephan. You have finally gotten your revenge and Rosie's.

Congratulations."

"Why are you still here? What else is there to do?" Stephan asked. The shadow grew larger, and came towards Stephan.

"There is only one thing left to do now, and deep down you know what that is. I'm not going to be the one to tell you." The demon reached out and touched his chest in the same place as it had done before when Stephan said its name. The same sites as before on his chest, burned like someone pouring drops of acid onto his bare skin. He backed away from the shadow with a glint of anger in his eyes.

"Quit doing that! What the hell are you trying to prove?" Stephan ordered angrily. The demon let out a hoarse, slow laugh.

"You will find out soon enough, Stephan. For now, I bid thee farewell, and I wish you the best of luck." The demon began to dissipate, but before it completely vanished, Stephan caught its final eerie message. "See you soon." It whispered. A shudder went through his entire body. What the shadow said confirmed what Stephan felt he must do, but his hereafter sounded doomed according to Orroth.

Stephan tried not to think about what was about to happen as he slowly made his way down the stairs. On his way down, he intercepted a young police officer and his seasoned partner. Stephan caught them off guard. He pointed the gun at them, and gave them both non-lethal shots in the shoulders that their bulletproof gear didn't cover. Stephan quickly reached down for their guns, and had them in his possession. "I don't wanna kill you or hurt you any more than I have to, because you guys are probably good guys that work hard. I just left some whiskey over there on that table, and I want to finish it before I surrender." Stephan sauntered over to the bottle, carrying the guns.

"Add this to a list of your charges." The young cop spat bitterly as he sat up against the wall clumsily, bleeding from his shoulder. He pressed his hand against his wound. His partner lay on the floor, moaning and mumbling profanities at Stephan.

"Officers, I don't intend on facing any charges any time soon. Ever hear of . . . going out with a bang?" Stephan sipped at the bottle at first. He watched the police outside through the living room window. "I killed the doctor's family . . . the Krocheks. I killed my ex-wife, and her lover upstairs." The police were preparing to come inside. "Your guns are right here on this table." He told the cops, and in one swig the bottle was empty. Stephan walked over by the officers, "you seem honest, and I trust you will know what to do with these." He threw the manila folders down in front of them. "Evidence against Euphoria Hills Institution . . . could be a big break for guys like you, especially since you got shot too." Stephan turned and walked to the front door with the loaded Beretta in hand. He stood in front of the door with his hand on the doorknob. This was it . . . how was this going to go? There was only one way it could go with him going outside, waving a loaded gun around in front of numerous police officers. He took a deep breath, and swung the door open. He pointed the gun at the police as walked hastily toward them, and when the armed men saw this, they wasted no time. They began to open fire. Stephan began to get hit with bullets. A pain that he had never felt before took over his body. A deep, aching, burning that felt like strong bee stings that had the intensity of electricity, penetrated his chest. He looked up to the sky and saw snow falling in slow motion. The second bullet took him to his knees and finally the third and fourth bullets lodged themselves in his heart and lung. He focused on a single snowflake before he closed his eyes and fell forward. Stephan Cranston was dead. Every place a bullet had hit him, was a place the demon's hand made the acidic burning sensation when it touched him. It was as if Orroth knew this was going to happen long before Stephan escaped from the hospital. It just needed him to finally give in.

The stinging pain lingered for a moment, but suddenly it was taken over by fading, dull aches. Stephan opened his eyes and looked around. For a moment, he thought that he had survived. Until he realized, he was looking down on his lifeless body lying face down in the front yard of his ex-wife's house. The police carefully approached his body with their guns still drawn, and pointed at him. He looked at the house, and then at the sky. Stephan was wondering how he was supposed to get to the light. He wanted to find Rosie. Everything around him grew darker like a vicious storm approaching. The voices of the police began to get more distant, and eventually faded away completely. Stephan found himself standing in front of the house alone in the darkening world. A familiar shadow began to form in front of him and fiery, red eyes opened. "Say my name." It ordered Stephan.

"Orroth." He answered, without hesitation. Stephan watched in numb silence as the shadow took the shape of the three headed, serpent-tailed beast as it had done before. It sat nude upon the bear, and had the sparrow hawk upon its wrist as it had before. The three heads began to speak at once to Stephan in harsh, raspy voice.

"I am Orroth. I was once in the Heavenly order, but then I was cast out along with Lucifer. I now command forty legions under the command of his infernal Majesty." Its eyes shot a circle of fire around Stephan, and trapped him within the fiery ring with the three headed demon along with him. He instantly forgot about trying to find the light and Rosie. "You, Stephan, will join my forty legions. You must honor the deal your father made."

"All this time, I wasn't crazy. I was just an asshole." Stephan mumbled. "What did my father get in return? I think I have the right to know that much." Stephan asked Orroth.

"He wanted your mother. She was going to take you and leave. He wouldn't have it. He traded you . . . for her to stay . . . and all it did was cause her hate him until the day she died, and he ended up leaving the two of you anyway.

Have you ever wondered why your father left after making the deal that he did?"

"I'm curious now." Stephan said.

"You think you're the only one who saw me? I told him that one day you would kill him, so he fled for his own life. Your father was a coward, through and through. You Stephan, you're not like him at all. You will do well serving me." At those words, the walls of the fire that surrounded them grew higher and more intense. Stephan knew he should have been afraid, but instead he felt an odd sense of power. He smiled at Orroth, opened his arms and closed his eyes. He started to laugh out loud as he began to step backwards slowly. He opened his eyes to look at the demon once more as the wild flames painlessly licked at his back. Stephan's eyes were like the fire that surrounded him. Orroth's bear growled ferociously and ran toward the fiery wall. It disappeared into the flames instantly. Stephan allowed himself to fall back into fire, and he joined the forty legions under Orroth's command.

CHAPTER 17

The storm was on the brink of calming down when the police arrived at the Krochek's residence. The discovery of the three victims was enough to sadden any veteran officer. Detectives had also made their way to the hospital, and found the bound Dr. Krochek in his office. When the news was delivered about his family, he didn't act surprised. He told the police that Stephan warned him of his intent, and he had rendered the doctor helpless. Stephan had come up with a dark plan, and he was determined to see it through. Dr. Krochek was still devastated, even though he knew his families fate before it had happened.

While Stephan was committing his crimes, the doctor had tried to escape to no avail. Eventually he sat and cried . . . a defeated and broken man. He felt what Stephan had felt in the very same chair only months before. He closed his eyes, and leaned his head back. He pictured his children's faces and his wife's smile. He felt a painful tightness in his chest that could only be described as heartbreak. The memories began to creep in his mind, and they made him cry harder. Dr. Krochek knew Stephan would follow through with what he said. He was desperate, and the doctor knew his diagnosis. Dr. Krochek also knew that Stephan was a man with nothing to lose now. He hoped that by some miracle that Stephan was bluffing. He prayed that he would leave his family alone, but it's not a perfect world.

The Lieutenant arrived, and approached Dr. Krochek. He observed the bleeding marks of struggling on the doctor's wrists. It was evident he tried to free himself away from the chair. He had the manila folders Stephan left with the wounded officers in his one hand. He had a small handheld device in his other hand. The Lieutenant barely looked at the doctor's face. Instead he read from the device, and observed the office.

"Victor Krochek. I just want you to know that this place is officially under investigation. We will be relocating your patients as soon as we can find a proper place for them all. Until then, we are going to get some new staff in here. You and your head nurse . . . Tracy Adams are both under investigation. As well as Stanley Montgomery . . . and Patricia Wagner, so don't any of you go very far. We're going to be in touch very soon, because we are going to have some questions. You be sure to tell Ms. Adams, Ms. Wagner and Mr. Montgomery not to go anywhere when you see them." The Lieutenant turned but looked at the doctor, "don't go anywhere, I want pictures of your wrists." Dr. Krochek's world instantly shattered around him again. His family was taken from him, and the experiment was over. Once the police read what was in those folders, Dr. Krochek, Nurse Adams, Dr. Montgomery and Dr. Wagner would be going to prison. The doctor didn't bring up the fact that Stephan called his desk phone. He wanted the police off of the hospital premises as soon as possible. Dr. Krochek was advised that he, and all the other doctors were not to treat any more patients, or conduct any more of the nocturnal experiment. He swore to obey.

The police left the office, but stationed two officers outside of the hospital.

Once everything calmed down, Dr. Krochek grabbed his extra key card from his filing cabinet. He began to look for Nurse Adams. The Nurse's Station was empty, but he managed to find other staff scattered around on the unit. No one had seen her for quite some time, which raised some concern. He began to frantically check every room. Out of desperation, he checked the closets, and began looking into patients' rooms. He stepped towards Stephan's old room, and opened the door halfway. He saw something laying on the floor. Dr. Krochek opened the door the rest of the way, and stepped toward the object. In a few steps, he realized what he was looking at. He fell to his knees, and slowly crawled towards her.

"Tracy!" He whispered a small shriek, as he shook her by her shoulders. With the shred of light that came in through the doorway, he saw the blood on her white uniform where Stephan had stabbed her repeatedly. He held his pointer and middle finger to the artery in her neck, but felt no sign of life. The light that dimly lit the room also gave him a good look at her ashen face. "I wish I could say I was sorry, but I think you're better off at this point." Dr. Krochek took his hand, closed her eyes, and smoothed her hair back. He let out a shaky sigh and stood up. He left the room and closed the door quietly behind him. He looked around at his surroundings, and smiled as he felt his heart drop into the depths of his stomach. He smiled at the thought that one patient like Stephan had gotten the best of him. One man ruined him and the hospital single handedly. Perhaps the smile was out of slight admiration for the tenacious, yet sinister man. Stephan did what Dr. Krochek would never have been able to do. The doctor made up his mind on what he must do next. He didn't bother to notify any of the staff about the dead nurse in the empty room. He lacked the ability to care at this point. Dr. Krochek made his way to the wide, double doors at the end of the corridor. He knew it was going to be the last time he would swipe his card to get off of the unit. He didn't bother to look back and see what he was leaving behind. Dr. Krochek knew his legacy was a failure now because of one man. He slowly walked to Dr. Montgomery's door, and pushed the button. The camera lens moved, and the intercom was fast to click on.

"Victor!" The voice of Dr. Montgomery was enthusiastically heard over the static speaker. The door was already opening without hesitation. When Dr. Montgomery looked closer at Dr. Krochek, he could tell something ominous was looming overhead. "Something happened . . . what?" Dr. Krochek stepped inside the office, and gently closed the door behind him.

"We should talk, Monty."

"This sounds serious." He went behind his desk, and removed his glasses. He retrieved a bottle of whiskey, and two dusty glasses from his desk's bottom drawer. Before Dr. Montgomery could start pouring, Dr. Krochek began to tell him the bad news.

"I feel you should know that you are under investigation as of today. The whole hospital is . . . Pat is . . . I am . . . Tracy is . . . was . . ." Dr. Krochek's voice trailed off.

"Was?" Dr. Montgomery questioned as he poured them each two fingers of whiskey.

"Stephan Cranston escaped last night. I spent most of the night . . . tied to a damn chair in my office trying to figure out how the hell he managed to do it."

"You didn't get a chance to ask?" Dr. Montgomery was surprised that his colleague wouldn't have inquired about such a feat.

"At the time, I guess it just didn't cross my mind. I suppose it would have something to do with this storm. Maybe it's the fact all I could focus on was the scalpel he had on me."

"I was in here while all that was happening?" He walked around the desk, and handed Dr. Krochek one of the glasses.

"He got out and killed Tracy, my wife and kids, and then he killed his ex-wife and Mr. S. He was sleeping with his ex-wife. Stephan tried to tell me, and I didn't listen. Maybe Stephan was right, a monkey *could* do this job better than me." Dr. Montgomery fell against his desk in a state of shock.

"They're all gone? I can't believe it. Victor . . . I'm so sorry, but you can't blame yourself for your family dying, or anything else that he did. You can't blame yourself for anything the mentally ill has done, especially when you have done so much to help them." Dr. Montgomery said, trying to raise his spirits.

"It's all over Monty. Everything we have tried to accomplish here, will have all been for nothing once they send their people in."

"Send *their* people in?"

"All new staff will be appointed by the state until a new facility can be found for the patients. Until then we are not to run the experiment, or be practicing doctors." Dr. Krochek took a long sip from his glass and looked at what he had left in it, and swirled dust particles around in the bottom with the whiskey. "Like I said, it's all over."

"Yeah . . . so what do you want to do with the time we have left?" Dr. Montgomery looked at Dr. Krochek with his vibrant, blue eyes, waiting for the next order. As far as he was concerned, he was still calling all the shots. Dr. Krochek looked at him with tired, sad eyes.

"I have a request that only a trusted friend could do for me, Monty." Dr. Krochek let out a sigh shakily.

"What would that be, Vic?"

"Put me in a machine. I want to be on that vacation I went on a few years ago, with her and the kids. When I'm under, and I am seeing them and holding them again . . . I need you to do me another . . . rather large favor."

"What kind of large favor, Vic." Dr. Montgomery's eyes didn't leave him. His gaze was intense as he wondered where his superior was going with his request. Dr. Krochek looked down at his whiskey again. He started to slowly, and continuously swirl it around in the bottom of the glass again.

"Give me enough morphine to take down an elephant." He whispered. Dr. Montgomery studied Dr. Krochek, and tried to establish if he was joking or not. All he saw was the desire brought on by a deep despair and failure. He had never seen a man so beaten down, and ready to let go of everything. There was no folly about what Victor Krochek asked his friend to do for him.

"I will oblige your wish's Vic . . . but not happily. I don't want to lose a friend." Dr. Montgomery whispered. He felt a lump form in his throat. "I suppose I can understand your pain though."

"Don't you see Monty? It's not just about my family, or the experiment . . . or even this place. It's over for you too. You're looking at prison. Stephan found my secret study at my home, and handed over every hidden document about this place to the police. Everything we've been hiding over the years. The deaths, neglect . . . all of it . . . and with your chiseled features, you'd never make it in prison. I'm sure you don't know how to fight to keep yourself alive, and I know I'm much too old for anything like that. As for Patricia, I haven't seen her to give her any kind of warning."

"Awww! Shit! I might as well join you . . . blow my brains out! Tracy is the lucky one!" The reality of the situation finally hit Stanley Montgomery. He downed the rest of his whiskey, and sloppily poured himself another glass with a shaking hand. He silently offered the bottle to Dr. Krochek, and he gratefully took it and topped off his drink.

"Stephan Cranston . . . the worst possible thing that ever happened to me. I should have let him go like he wanted." Dr. Krochek said thoughtfully, as he sipped his whiskey like a gentlemen.

"You had no way of knowing that any of this would happen. Horrible circumstances . . . brought on by his actions."

"He did it, because that girl died . . . Rosalie Carmichael. Those two had gotten pretty close during their short time here. She was a rebound because his wife divorced him, but it's what he needed at the time. I don't know how they managed to do it, but he got her pregnant." Dr. Krochek told Dr. Montgomery.

"I knew about the pregnant patient. I didn't know the baby was his and any of this would come from one patient dying."

"Yeah well it did. Let's get this show on the road before their workers show up and take over." Dr. Krochek rushed to finish his drink at that point. Dr. Montgomery finished his in one gulp, and went to his top desk drawer and retrieved a key. He walked over to the medical supply closet in the corner and unlocked it. He grabbed two bottles of liquid morphine, a bottle filled with a milky solution with no label, and a clean syringe wrapped in plastic. He put the contents in the front pocket of his white coat and locked the cabinet. He returned the key to its rightful place in his desk drawer. He looked at Dr. Krochek and nodded his head. The two men headed out of the office, and toward the second set of double doors that led to the Control Rooms.

"You're sure this is the way you wanna do this?" Dr. Montgomery asked, hoping to coax his friend out of the finality of death.

"What other way is there? It's the closest thing I have to being with my family, and it's quick and painless." They went into Control Room 3, and went to the only empty bed. Perhaps the doctor would have reconsidered this if he remembered who was lying in the bed hours before. Dr. Krochek pulled a picture of his family out of his pocket. It was the same picture Stephan had mocked earlier in his office. When the police untied him, the doctor removed it from the frame. He kept it close to him to keep it from being desecrated any further. He looked at the photo, and remembered asking the stranger to take the picture for them that day at the beach. The four of them huddled together around an epic sand castle that they had spent three hours building. The children had proud, excited smiles on their faces, and everyone was happy. It was a beautiful, warm day at the beach, captured in time forever. "This day . . . give me this Monty. Please." Dr. Krochek kissed the picture, and a tear slid down his cheek. He laid down quickly, and took a deep breath. "I'll be there soon guys." He whispered.

"How do you know people like us go to Heaven?" Dr. Montgomery asked softly, as he got the machine ready.

"I wasn't a bad person. We were doing this for all the right reasons." Dr. Krochek said, trying to convince himself.

"Maybe you should make peace with our maker while I do this. Your wife was a good woman, and your kids were innocent. Just be sure your seat up there is reserved Vic. That's all I'm saying."

"I'm sure there is plenty of room, and I'm sure my baby put in a good word for me." Dr. Krochek adjusted himself on the bed to get comfortable. He folded his hands on his stomach with the picture, and waited patiently.

"All right, if you think now is the best time to be proud . . . go for it." Dr. Montgomery mumbled as he continued to tap buttons on the flat screen. After fifteen minutes of tapping, a long sequence of beeps was heard. "The machine is ready for you, Vic." Dr. Krochek sat up, removed his white coat, and folded it neatly so his stitched name showed on top. He revealed a short sleeve lavender button down. He laid back down, and allowed the machine to move over with its mechanical arm, hover over his head, and drop down. The metal brackets forced his eyes open, and the metal plates suctioned themselves to his head. The tubes began to lubricate his eyes immediately.

"This is an awful feeling. The patients were lucky to be drugged. OOOHHH! I almost can't stand it! Hurry UP!" Dr. Krochek growled from in between his teeth. He felt a cold, damp pad cleaning the inside of his arm.

"I'm about to give you the medication to put you under so you can see your alternate reality. It will kick in fast, because of the dose I'm giving you." Dr. Montgomery said gently. "Goodbye, my friend. Godspeed." He stuck the needle into the top of the vial that contained the milky solution, and filled the syringe. He stuck the needle into the vein of Dr. Krochek's arm, and released the medication with the plunger.

"Thank you, Monty. I'll never forget that you did this for me." Dr. Montgomery grabbed hold of his colleagues hand and clenched his jaw to keep the tears from falling. Dr. Krochek started feeling the effects of the medication that he was given right away, and he let himself drift away.

Victor went to the Costa Rican coast with his family. They spent the morning body surfing, and gathering broken seashells in a plastic, yellow bucket. Before they ate lunch, the four of them walked the surf together. Victor and his son began to play tag, and splash one another. Finally, Victor went up to his son and grabbed him, and hoisted him onto his shoulders. The young boy giggled with glee, and intertwined his fingers together over his father's forehead. They ate picnic lunch of ham sandwiches, potato chips and cold cans of soda. Victor and his wife laid in the sun lazily as they watched their children kick a ball back and forth further down by the water. Victor suddenly had a brilliant idea looking at the bucket full of seashells.

"Hey guys!" He hollered to his children to come to him. They grabbed their ball, and obediently came running. "Do you guys want to build an amazing sand castle? We can use the seashells we gathered to decorate it." Both of the children's eyes lit up, and they started to jump up and down excitedly. The four of them found the perfect spot closer to the water, and they began to build the epic sand castle from the picture. They included tall towers and a water filled moat surrounding a wall. It felt good not to be Dr. Krochek again, he was simply 'daddy' and 'honey'. Victor was enjoying being in a simpler, less complicated time. He didn't have gray hair today. He was a much younger man and his wife was younger. Their children were at the age where they still wanted to cuddle up to their mom and dad, and be playful. They finally finished the sand castle as the sun was beginning to set, and the tide began to gracefully roll in. Victor asked the stranger to use his phone to capture this moment in time, and his wife would print it out later. They gathered around the castle, and all gave their bright smiles on sun kissed faces. It would become Vic's favorite family photo. Relaxed, yet intimate, and it showed the innocence of the world they were living in at the time. They stayed on the beach as the sun set, and the stars came out. They weren't worried about dinner tonight. Victor wanted to stay on the beach for as long as possible. The tide destroyed the sand castle, and the children curled up on their parents' laps, and fell asleep under their beach towels. Victor and his wife combed their fingers through the children's hair. They enjoyed the feeling of the warm sand beginning to cool beneath their bodies and the sound of the rolling waves, until his wife whispered to him.

"My darling, look, shooting stars." Mrs. Krochek pointed toward the sky.

Victor looked up, and saw the stars falling to the earth like meteors. They began to crash into the ocean, and all around them causing massive explosions.

"I love you." Victor said, looking at his wife, with a tinge of fear in his eyes. He held on tightly to his sleeping son, and grabbed her hand. At that, his world ended. The beach, the ocean, and the Krocheks were gone, and everything faded to black.

Dr. Montgomery stood over Dr. Krochek in Control Room 3. He ran his fingers through his thick, black hair and sobbed quietly for a moment, but just as quick as the tears were brought on, they were replaced by laughter. He put the used syringe and three empty bottles medication into his front pocket. He let out a long sigh, and turned off the machine that the doctor was hooked up too. The mechanical arm took the machine away from Dr. Krochek's head. Dr. Montgomery looked at his colleague's open eyes and smiled. With one hand he reached out, and closed them out of respect. He exited the room, and walked back to his office. Once he was back in the room, he sat behind his desk. He opened the bottle of Jack Daniels, and retrieved his bourbon glass from before. He paused for a moment, and looked sadly at the glass Dr. Krochek drank out of not too long before. He quickly looked away, filled his halfway and started to sip at the strong drink. In the same drawer he had gotten the whiskey and glasses from earlier, also sat a locked metal box. Before he could even delve into the box, he needed to do something first. He pulled some paper with a pen out of his top drawer, and began to write a letter. Dr. Montgomery thought everything needed to be seen from his point view, even if it was through a letter. He wanted to make sure everything would be all right for his brother, Paul Montgomery.

To Whom It May Concern,

I have no wife or children. I don't think I'll be able to rightfully ask for anything of mine to be donated to a charity of my choice. My assets will more than likely all be seized with the evidence the police will find against me. That's not the reason for this letter though. I need to make peace with what I did. What WE ALL did. Not just with God, but with any of the families that care about what happened to their loved ones. All I can say is, I'm sorry. I was not the brain behind the operation, but I won't deny my part either. I'm not going to point blame or mention any names, but my own. In the beginning, we were doing this for the right reasons. Everything just got so out of control, and when the government's money started coming in . . . things really started changing then. The money started to speak more then the knowledge we were seeking. I don't know what else to say. I have no excuse for what we did. We did some things wrong. I guess we did a lot of things wrong, and it took a man like Stephan Cranston to point that out, and finally end our wrongdoings. Either way, it's over now, and I have no way of making it up to any of the people hurt in the process.

My dearest Paul, I'm sorry you had to become a pawn in this. I never should have let them do this to you. I don't know how I could have let my own brother take part in the experiment. I'll never forgive myself for letting you get caught up in this mess. Meg, sweet sister of ours, please make sure to take care of Paul. Let him do what will make him happy, no matter how painful it is to accept. I'm sorry I'm not the person whom you thought I was. I let you both down, and I can't express how sorry I am. I love you both, but I would never make it in prison.

I love you, and I'm sorry.

Best Regards,
The Former
Dr. Stanley "Monty" Montgomery

He shakily put the pen down, and moved the letter to the far side of the desk. He searched for his car keys in the top drawer, and located a small key on it. Dr. Montgomery leaned over, retrieved the box from the desk drawer, and placed it directly in front of him. He grabbed his whiskey, and took a long drink from the glass. He took the little key, and unlocked the box. Inside, neatly fit a loaded Browning 1911-380 Black Label Pro semi automatic pistol, wrapped in a soft cloth. It held eight rounds, but he only needed one for what he was going to do. Dr. Montgomery gingerly pulled the material away from the gun, and ran his finger across the stainless steel and black finish before he carefully pulled it from the box. He clicked the safety off, and the gun was now ready to fire. He placed the gun on his desk and continued to sip at his whiskey a bit more. He poured a little more Jack into his glass, and walked over to the corner. He turned on the radio. A Classic Rock station was playing, and he decided to leave it there. He sat back down at his desk and began to slowly finish his drink. He put his hand over the loaded gun.

"Oh, God! I don't wanna go . . . but what other choice is there? All the things I've done." He pounded his other fist on the arm of his desk chair. He started to laugh, but it began to sound like sobs. He ran his fingers through his short, straight hair, and it stood straight up. "God, is this my life? Is this how it really ends? I thought I had more to offer." Dr. Montgomery poured himself another drink, and had it all finished at once. He was starting to feel the effects of the alcohol. He leaned forward towards the desk, and was jabbed by something in his coat. "Ouch! What the . . .?" He remembered the syringe and the three empty bottles of medicine in his pocket. "Oh God! Forgive me, please! I'm begging for you to show me mercy when the time comes for my judgment. I have spilled so much blood. How could you ever forgive a murderer like me? I couldn't even deny Vic, and I knew it was wrong." He drank more whiskey straight from the bottle. He was feeling very much inebriated after that. "Fuck it, maybe I actually deserve Hell, and if that's the case . . . so did the rest of them. See ya there Vic! I know you're there with Stephan, and he's probably making you his bitch by now. We all deserve it." Dr. Montgomery looked at the gun, raised it, and placed it against the side of his head. He closed his eyes, and breathed out one last time before he squeezed the trigger. The bullet penetrated the temple, and ricocheted inside his skull. Dr. Montgomery died instantly.

"I will make it go away! Can't be here no more! Seems this is the only way! I will soon be gone! These feelings will be gone! These feelings will be gone! . . . Now I see the times they change. Leaving doesn't seem so strange . . ." The radio continued to play as the doctor lay slumped on his desk with his gun and letter next to him. *"All the s#*t I seem to take. All alone I seem to break. I have lived the best I can . . ."* Jonathon Davis sang through the antique radio's speakers. Detectives would have no problem seeing this was a suicide, and why he did it. It was just a matter of when the bodies were going to be found. No one was around to hear the gun shot. No one knew Dr. krochek was dead in Control Room 3. The one person who knew was not going to say a word. No one knew Nurse Adams was laying dead in Stephan's old room. Even after his death, Stephan was still managing to cause chaos.

CHAPTER 18

Nine months have passed, and the state had seized complete control over the hospital for months. The police were keeping a close eye on the place as well. A black McLaren 570GT slowly rolled up to the front of Euphoria Hills Institution. A woman with dark brown hair got out. She wore a short and classy black dress with modest, two inch heels. She immediately caught the attention of a young, rookie officer. He stopped writing on his tablet, and tipped his hat to her.

"Can I help you miss?"

"Yes, I was told that some of the patients were relocated. Was one of them named Stephan Cranston by any chance, and where was he placed?"

"Stephan Cranston!" The cop gave her a look of utter disbelief. "You haven't heard? He's the reason all this went down. He killed a bunch of people, and then he got shot to death himself." The woman put her hand on her chest, and let out a short gasp. "Are you all right? How did you not know about this? It's been the biggest thing going on for months now. That guy blew this whole place apart, and now it's under investigation. There are state workers in there now and . . ." He moved closer to her, and hushed his tone. "The workers found the doctor responsible for it all . . . dead in his own virtual reality experiment. Found the head nurse . . . dead in Cranston's old room. We're all betting Cranston did that one, and then there's the doctor that blew his head off in his office, instead of facing prison. It's been crazy. The doctor we haven't found . . . Wagner . . . we think she skipped town. Somehow, someone tipped her off. We're thinking she had some money stashed, and she fled the country. We just don't know who tipped her off."

"I've been out of the country on business. So, keeping up with the news here in the states was not a luxury I had where I was located." She paused, and took in a long, deep breath. "Thank you for your assistance officer."

"You're welcome . . . Uh, Miss . . . What was your relationship to Mr. Cranston?"

"I was just a friend . . . and I was concerned about him being here to begin with . . . but maybe he's happier wherever he is now."

"What's your name?"

"Sophia Murray." She answered. The officer gave her grin and tipped his hat. She smiled and nodded. She turned on her heel to get back into the car. At that moment, a truck came barreling down the driveway, and the weathered man behind the wheel did a double take of the dark-haired woman. She gave a short wave and small smile. The man driving the truck stopped the truck and rolled down the window. Sophia walked over to the truck.

"Hello again, Pete." She said quietly.

"I see you have made it. I'm happy to see you doing well." He responded as he reached his hand through the open window. He took her hand in his. "I'm sorry about your friend." He said sincerely. She swallowed a lump in her throat, and blinked back hot tears. After a few minutes, she managed to compose herself.

"I have a feeling, you know about Dr. Wagner . . . would I be wrong?" She asked Pete.

"Nurse Adams and Dr. Krochek thought she didn't know who I was. They were wrong. She was the only one who treated me like I was more than broke maintenance man in the basement. She treated me with nothing but kindness. Nurse Adams and Dr. Krochek treated me like vermin." He sighed and stared through the windshield longingly. "The thing about vermin is they see and hear everything. I chose to give Dr. Wagner a warning when Stephan stole my truck. I knew it wasn't going to end well. She chose not to warn the others." He smiled and looked over at Sophia. "I suppose I've kept you long enough."

"Thank you, for everything Pete." She reached into her purse and pulled out her checkbook. "Before you go, let me pay you back." She began to write a check for two hundred thousand dollars.

"That's not necessary. I was just glad to help."

"I insist. With this money . . . get away from here. You will be free and you can live comfortably." She handed him the check along with her business card. "If you ever need anything, call me. I'm seriously . . . forever in your debt." The woman quickly turned towards her car before Pete could resist. "Bye Pete." She said quietly with a small wave. He waved back at her and continued down the driveway, never to return to the hospital again.

Sophia sat in her driver seat and buckled the seat belt. She turned to the passenger seat, and smiled. "How about it munchkin, are you ready to hit the road? Wanna go home?" She reached over, and offered her finger for a tiny hand to grasp. A baby boy in a car seat smiled. His dark eyes peeked out from dark curls. "Mommy loves you, Stephan!" The little baby in the car seat looked admirably at his mother. You could see a fire in his eyes that you saw only in one other person. Sophia put the car in drive, and put the hospital behind her. She refused to look at the broken building in the rear view mirror. Her dark wavy curls billowed in the wind from the open window. She was going to make a home for herself, and her son. She already had a good start at a new life. One of many talks she had with a dear friend, had led her to bringing her idea for an invention to life that made her millions.

Sophia drove back to the city where she had a penthouse suite with her and little Stephan's belongings packed. Everything was ready to go. The plan was to pick up Stephan and leave, but fate played the cards differently. Sadly, it would only be she and the little one. Sophia thought about how nice it would've been to surprise Stephan with his son he never knew he had. Maybe he wouldn't have reacted the way he did that night. It made her sad to think that Stephan felt that killing was the only way he had out. She wished she could talk to him one more time. She wanted to ask him why he felt he had to kill the doctor's family. She already had pretty good idea why he killed his ex-wife. Why couldn't he have waited? She could've talked him out of doing what he did, and they could have lived happily, away from the people that made them miserable. Sophia didn't know the whole story of what Stephan did that night, and she didn't want to . . . she wanted to remember him as he was, and not for what he had become out of ignorance.

EPILOGUE

"This patient looks like she's gaining weight." Nurse Adams suggested quietly to Dr. Krochek. They both looked at her chart. "She hasn't been menstruating either . . . how have we missed this? She's pregnant, I just know it!"

"See how far along she is, if she is." Dr. Krochek ordered calmly. Nurse Adams left the control room quickly and obeyed her orders. She had the results for Dr. Krochek within a half hour. She quickly marched back to his office and rang his intercom. The camera moved to see who it was, and the door automatically opened. She pushed her way through, rushed and on the edge.

"Sir, she's four months along . . . this could end us." Nurse Adams said frantically. Dr. Krochek thought for a moment.

"You know what to do." He gave her a knowing look, and she responded with a silent nod of her head. She left Dr. Krochek's office, and headed straight for Dr. Montgomery's office. He opened his door to her immediately, and she slammed the door behind her. She looked at him with a pale face. Her words were jittery, but she managed to get them out.

"Monty, we have a problem. A patient is pregnant, and Dr. Krochek has asked me to take care of the problem." He could tell her nerves were shot over the situation.

"Now, calm down." Dr. Montgomery went to his bottom desk drawer and brought out a bottle of whiskey and two glasses. He poured a finger's worth in each glass and handed one of the drinks to Nurse Adams. "Here . . . this should help settle your nerves a bit." She gratefully took it, and finished it all at once. She handed the empty glass back to Dr. Montgomery who placed it on the desk.

"How do you propose you take care of . . . this problem?" He finally asked her.

"He left it up to my imagination, which is why I'm here. I need a bottle of morphine, and a syringe. That should take care of her, and then cremate her in the basement."

"I suppose that could work . . . I hope you're planning on covering the rest . . . like no paper trail. It has to be like she was never here." Dr. Montgomery made his way to the cabinet in the corner and unlocked it. He retrieved a bottle of liquid morphine and a clean syringe, and handed them to Nurse Adams.

"Oh, it will be as if she was here, she has family. She tragically died from an allergic reaction to medication. Trust me, if you think for a second, I'm going to let, some pregnant harlet . . . ruin this hospital, and what we are trying to accomplish, you're sadly mistaken." She whirled around quickly, and hastily made her way to Control Room 1 where Rosalie lie in her alternate reality.

"I don't know how you two managed to do it . . . but you were bound and determined to bring this place down, one way or another." Nurse Adams said to Rosie, as she dreamed deeply. "Now look at what I have to do. I have to kill you . . . and your child, because you fell under that misfits spell. What a shame." Nurse Adams gave her a small dose of sedative to keep her asleep, and unhooked her from the catheter and the monitors she was hooked up to. She disconnected her virtual reality machine last. It rose up and away from Rosie's head. Nurse Adams fetched the empty Gurney from against the wall and wheeled it against Rosie's bed. She locked the wheels and began to lift the top half of Rosie onto the other Gurney first. Then she got her hips and legs over. She covered her over with a sheet and wheeled her out of the room. She made her way with Rosie down the hallway. She went through both sets of double doors, and into the cafeteria.

Nurse Adams took her into the elevator, and downstairs into the basement where she and her babies fate was sealed.

Down in the basement, Nurse Adams wheeled the Gurney under a bright light that hung from the ceiling. She went to pull the small glass bottle of morphine from her pocket, but it slipped from her fingers. It shattered to pieces when it hit the concrete floor.

"Dammit!" She yelled out of frustration. Pete Majors poked his head from around his doorway.

"Something I can do to help?" He stepped out of the room and approached her slowly. Nurse Adams eyed Pete up and down thoughtfully.

"Come here." She hissed. Pete quickly and nervously did as he was told.

"You've worked and lived here for quite some time."

"Yes Ma'am." Pete said, keeping his head down.

"So, I'm sure I can trust you with a task that may question ones morals just a bit . . ."

"Absolutely. I would do anything for this place. It's my home. You and Dr. Krochek have been so gracious to let me live here, and never said a word."

"Well, it's a basement. I suppose it's perfect for someone like you. You're like a cockroach, and you crave living among filth." She studied Pete.

"You're right Ma'am. Vermin live in filth too . . . some of the most cunning creatures. That's how you know you can trust me with whatever you need, Ma'am."

"I like your point." Nurse Adams sighed, and pulled the sheet back to bare Rosie in a deep sleep. "I need her cremated as soon as possible. Waste no time. There is a possibility of her waking since I dropped the morphine, and can't give it to her. The cremation furnace will do the job nicely." Nurse Adams ordered gently, putting her hand on his.

"Yes Ma'am! You can count on me!" He said enthusiastically. Nurse Adams turned, and took the stairs back up to the kitchen to begin the paperwork on the matter. What she didn't know is that Pete watched her drop the bottle, and saw the girl had a chance to get out. He had no intent of doing what Nurse Adams told him to do. He picked Rosie up from the Gurney and laid her in his bed. He completely covered her up. He lit the fire in the retort, and grabbed his bow and arrow. He was gone

169

for forty-five minutes, and had two deer with him when he returned. The fire was hot enough to burn anything by now. He threw the two deer onto the steel slab and rolled them into the fiery, cremation chamber and closed the door. It was time to let the flames do their job.

A half hour later, Nurse Adams came back for the Gurney. Pete was found standing by the cremation furnace.

"Has it been done?" She asked earnestly.

"Yep." Pete answered simply. She saw the red, hot flames licking through the slots of the chamber door. She could have sworn she caught a glimpse of a bone. When she saw that, she had to quickly look away. She composed herself, and looked at Pete.

"A job well done, but this never happened." She said in a hushed tone.

"I know." Pete replied. Nurse Adams grabbed the Gurney, and took the elevator back upstairs. When he heard the elevator doors open in the kitchen, he waited ten minutes to be sure Nurse Adams was off doing something else. He didn't want her coming back to bother him. Pete went back to his room, and checked on the woman he had in his bed. She was starting to come around, but was still groggy. He wasn't aware of what they were doing to the patients upstairs. He knew that when they came downstairs, it was because it didn't go well for that patient upstairs. He saw one he could save, and that's what he was going to do. Pete kept watch over Rosie all night, only dozing off a couple of times in his chair. When she woke in the morning, she was a bit confused and felt like she drank a liquor store. Pete fed her, and gave her what clothes he could find that would fit her. He didn't have much money, but he managed to be able to give her two hundred and seventy-five dollars, and for that she was grateful.

When he was ready to make his daily run for errands into town, he had Rosie sit on the passenger seat floor of his truck. He told her to stay as low as possible. When he asked her where she wanted him to take her . . . she told him to drop her off at the county line. She figured she would be out of danger there. He wished her well, and she kissed the weathered cheek of her savior. He drove away, and watched Rosie disappear in his rear view mirror. He felt terrible leaving her like that with very little money, and nothing else but the clothes on her back, especially since she confided in him that she felt like she was pregnant. She said she could feel something moving. He told her that every woman would know if they were pregnant . . . at

170

least that's what his mother said when she told him she was pregnant with his sister when he was five years old. If she went to the next county over, she could get help with fewer questions being asked. Pete went about his usual tasks, but not without saying a quick, silent prayer for the woman he rescued.

Rosie's first move was to stop at a drug store. She bought some cheap, ammonia free coloring for her hair. Her second move was to find an affordable motel. She found one that rented by the week at a rate of seventy dollars. Rosie dyed her hair in the bathroom. When she was finished, she used the blow dryer attached to the wall and dried her hair. She stared in the mirror and got a good look at herself.

"Hmm, who knew I would look so damn good as a brunette." She said out loud. She needed a new name for herself. She would think of that later, right now she needed to use the phone. She went over to the night stand, and hit the yellow page's button on the phone. An automated voice began to speak.

"Thank you for choosing yellow pages. What type of business are you looking for?"

"Free clinic." After some aggravation with the automated yellow pages, Rosie finally got the number for the free clinic for the county she was in. She hung up the phone, picked it back up, and called the clinic. Someone answered after the third ring. "I think I'm pregnant, I need an appointment." Rosie told the woman on the other end.

"Do you have insurance?" The woman asked blandly on the other end.

"No. If I did, I would go to someone else."

"Well, you can come in whenever you like. We don't make appointments."

"Where are you located?" After receiving the location, Rosie hung up the phone. Tomorrow she was going to find out if her hunch was correct. Luckily, the clinic she was going to, catered to those without insurance. She would have to fill the documents under a false name.

Rosie decided to take a walk to see what she could find. She found a clothing store, and bought a new outfit. She went back to her motel room, and put it on. When she looked in the mirror, she couldn't help but give herself a half smile. She looked like any other woman you would see out in the world, and she hadn't felt that in a long time. Rosie remembered seeing a cemetery with some older looking headstones on her travels into the county. She decided to go back out and look at the headstones for a new identity. When she entered the cemetery, she could tell it was a bit unkempt. The grass hadn't been mowed in awhile, and weeds were starting to become overgrown. Rosie went to the most dilapidated headstones. The ones that looked like no one had cared for them in years and she started to read names. 'Martha Akers . . . No.' She moved to the next one. 'Sophia Murray. I could live with that.' She cleared the grass and weeds, and looked at the dates located lower on the headstone. The death date was before her birth date. She needed to find someone who specialized in documents. She needed an identification card at least.

The next morning Rosie woke up, took a shower and put her new outfit on. She didn't sleep well. Strange dreams woke her up continuously. Her memory began to come back, and she remembered everything from before she was put under. She remembered Stephan, and she was worried about him. She figured he must have gotten caught not taken his pills, and was stuck in his own nocturnal state. Rosie knew she would have to get him out somehow.

She had the directions to the clinic, and she began the one and a half mile walk to her destination. It took her almost two hours to get there. She went through the door, and had to use her finger to sign her name into a tablet that was linked to a television on the wall. She looked around the waiting room. There were only two people ahead of her. She wouldn't have to wait long. Rosie took a seat and waited patiently and cautiously.

"Brittany P.," a woman came out of an office and announced the name that came up on the television. A woman sitting across from Rosie, gathered her purse, a diaper bag and her toddler. She followed the woman into an office. Rosie rested her head back against the wall, and closed her eyes. She remembered Stephan again. She thought about him being locked away in the hospital still. Now that the impossible had happened for her, she had to get him out. 'What plan could I come up with to get him out? What would Stephan do?' She thought to herself

"Sophia M.," the woman said impatiently. She had called Rosie three times. She was daydreaming, and had tuned everything out. She got up quickly, and went with the woman to the office. "Have you ever been here before?"

"No," Rosie answered.

"Insurance?"

"I don't have any."

"Do you have an ID card?" She asked, starting to sound even more annoyed.

"No. I forgot it at home." Rosie replied, thinking quickly.

"What's your name then?" The woman looked at Rosie.

"Sophia Murray."

"Date of birth?"

"March 14, 2055." Rosie said, using the date from the headstone with her birth year.

"Address?"

"The Green Light Motel. Room 8." The woman looked at Rosie for a couple of seconds before she put the data into the system.

"I'm assuming your phone number would be the motel then. Nothing more permanent?"

"Yes, that's as permanent as it gets right now." Rosie responded.

"What brings you here today?"

"I think I'm pregnant."

"Okay." The woman put the data into the hologram computer. She tried to hide the pity in her eyes. "Have a seat in the waiting room and we'll call you back shortly." The woman said sweetly, suddenly changing her tone toward her. Rosie got up, went back into the waiting room, and sat down. Again, she rested her head against the wall, and closed her eyes. She tried to figure out how she could get Stephan out of the hospital. She thought Pete could help, but then she thought it would be too much to ask after everything he had done already. Other people got called back, and soon more people shuffled in to be seen, and the waiting room filled up rapidly.

"Sophia Murray." Rosie stood up, and followed behind a nurse. She walked her back to an exam room. The nurse closed the door behind them. "All right, so you think you're pregnant." The nurse opened a cabinet door, and pulled out a device. She put a tab over a sensor, and turned it on. She took an alcohol pad, and cleaned the tip of Rosie's finger. She pricked it with a device that looked like a pen with a sharp needle inside of it, and squeezed the blood onto the tab she put over the sensor. When the tab was filled in red, the nurse quit squeezing, and put a band-aid on Rosie's finger. The device made a long beep, and printed out a piece of paper with a plus sign and some numbers. "Well, congratulations, you are pregnant. Four months it would appear. Let me give these results to the doctor, and she will be back to talk to you in just a few minutes. Congratulations!" The nurse cleaned up the device, and gathered what she needed for the doctor. As soon as the nurse left, Rosie left unseen out of the building. She found out what she needed to know. She didn't need prenatal advice from a doctor, especially now since she was living in a motel room. She was also technically dead. She had no identity. How could a woman like that have, and raise children? She couldn't have a real life. She found herself walking passed the local high school. It was lunch time, and some of the kids were eating outside. Without thinking, Rosie approached a group of kids sitting at a picnic table under a large oak tree.

"Hey, I was wondering if any of you know where I could get a fake ID?" The kids looked at each other, and laughed quietly among themselves.

"Are you like a cop or something, because if you are, you have to like . . .

tell us?" One boy said, as he swept his long bangs off to the side.

"I'm not a cop, just looking for someone with skills in faking legal documentation, like identification."

"I call cop." A girl chimed in. Rosie sighed with disgust, and placed her head in one of her hands.

"Do you think I *like* having to come to a bunch of kids for something like this?" Silence ensued among the group for a moment.

"I could probably hook you up. It'll cost you though." One boy finally said without looking up from his phone. His friends whispered incoherently at him. "How much?" Rosie asked. The boy looked her up and down.

"Forty bucks . . . non-negotiable."

"All right, it's a deal, but you get the cash when I'm satisfied with what I get."

"Okay . . . playing a little hard ball, but it's a deal." Rosie and the boy shook on it. "Put my number in your cell. Get a hold of me when you're ready."

"I don't have a cell, write your number down, and I'll call you from my motel room."

"Damn, you must be in some shit. No phone . . . motel room. What's your story? You a fugitive or something? What are you running from?" A girl asked.

"Trust me, my story should stay unknown." Rosie mumbled. She grabbed the piece of paper with the boy's number on it, and left without saying another word.

Rosie waited until almost four to call the number. She knew school would be out by that time. She dialed the number on the motel phone, and a youthful male voice picked up on the third ring.

"This is Sophia, the woman who approached you during your lunch today."

"Oh, right. If you need it that soon, I can probably get it tonight. What motel are you staying at?"

"The Green Light."

"I can be there in fifteen minutes." The kid hung up abruptly. Rosie went outside and waited for him to arrive. Fifteen minutes later, a loud, red car pulled up, and the kid from earlier poked his head out of the driver side window. "Your chariot, my lady." He said, with a goofy grin. Rosie slid into the low passenger seat, and put the seatbelt on.

"So, you know someone seriously . . . right? This isn't some set up in your friend's basement ran by his older brother, is it?" Rosie asked suspiciously.

"I understand why you would have your doubts, but hey . . . I'll just say, I know people. Let's just leave it at that." They drove for twenty minutes out to the middle of nowhere. They approached an old farmhouse, and the kid slowed down. He pulled into the neat, gravel driveway, and cut the engine. "Things are about to get loud and a little crazy." They both got out of the car and went to the front door. He didn't bother ringing the bell or knocking. The kid walked in like it was his home. When those inside took a look at whom it was, he was greeted warmly. Cheerful, welcoming shouts were heard coming from inside. Rosie timidly stepped inside, but stayed in the background.

"Hey, hey! Look who it is!" One man said.

"This knucklehead is too busy chasing tail to come 'round here anymore." Another man said.

"To what do we owe the pleasure?" Another man finally asked. The kid motioned for Rosie to come into the room where the men were sitting around a card table playing five card stud.

"Who is this lovely lady?"

"This is Sophia. She needs some identification documents." He turned away from Rosie, and quieted his voice. "I believe funds are limited, so this would be more of a favor to me." The man thought about it for a moment as chewed on the end of a cigar.

"What's your last name, Sophia?"

"Murray." The man pulled the cigar from his mouth, and studied Rosie intently. He got a small smile on his face.

"Let's get you legal." The cigar wielding man finally said. He took her to a large basement where there were numerous machines. One was for counterfeiting paper currency, and it was loaded with one hundred dollar plates. There was another that made legitimate driver's license, and identification cards. There were presses that specialized in printing savings bonds among many other things that would have any federal court judge drooling.

"I can trust that since I'm doing this for you that everything you see down here will be forgotten upon exiting this house." The man said as he positioned her for the driver's license photo.

"I'm not going to say anything. You seem to be a man who likes to make money. I can respect that and who am I to interfere?" Rosie whispered.

"That's a great answer. Considering I know your real name isn't Sophia Murray. I've seen that headstone in that cemetery, because I played there as a boy. Are you in some kind of trouble?" He asked her quietly.

"I . . ." She hesitated.

"I'm not going to say anything. Look around you. Do I look like the kind of person to tell on someone?"

"I suppose you wouldn't." He snapped her picture, and started to print her new drivers license. "I escaped from Euphoria Hills . . . a nurse was going to kill me, because I'm pregnant." Rosie explained further about the experiment. He was told about Stephan and how he was still at the hospital.

"I'm glad I helped you. For once all this stuff comes in handy for a noble cause." The man said. He caught Rosie looking at the machines around the basement. "You like to make money?" He asked her.

"Depends on the business. I'm more like an idea person. So, I would need someone who could back that up. Someone who knows how to run a business, and could lend a few bucks until I could pay it back." Rosie said coyly. The man laughed heartily and raised his eyebrows at her.

"You're all right, I like you." The man told her. That night she became Sophia Murray. She acquired a birth certificate, a social security card and number, a driver's license, and a certificate for a completed GED. She paid the kid his forty bucks, and thanked him. Rosie didn't ask questions about how a kid his age knew men like that. Some things are better left unknown. She went back to her motel room, and held her new life on paper in her hands as Sophia Murray. This was the name she would give when she would introduce herself or fill out a job application. Now she would be able to pick up the pieces of her life, and put it all back together. She knew she was in for a lot of hard work, but it wasn't just about her. She had a baby on the way. She also had to think about getting Stephan out, but she wanted to have something for him to come out to, instead of being stuck like she was. Rosie had some ideas that would make lots of money. Maybe she could bring one of her ideas to life, and finally profit from it. Maybe she could be one of the lucky ones that turned a pipedream into a reality.

Printed in the United States
By Bookmasters